P9-BYW-793

"**Here's the thing—I may not have bargained on being a father but now that it's staring me in the face, then I intend to accept responsibility fully and without compromise.**

"Full-time fatherhood. One hundred percent involvement. I won't be conveniently disappearing, leaving you to carry on and do your own thing. I happen to place a great deal of worth on the importance of being an engaged parent!"

Violet knew that her mouth was hanging open. She'd never heard Matt talk like this before, not in this tone, not with this urgency or searing honesty. His eyes were blazing and angry. Although, she really had no idea what, exactly, he was trying to say. Did he want to sort out visiting rights here and now? Maybe get her to sign something? Or worse...

"I'm not going to hand my baby over to you, Matt..." She blanched, sick at the thought that this might end up as a fight through the courts with an innocent baby as the end prize.

"Did you hear me ask you to?"

"Then I don't understand what you're trying to say."

"Marriage, Violet. A ring on your finger and a walk up the aisle. That's where I'm going with this."

Cathy Williams can remember reading Harlequin books as a teenager, and now that she is writing them, she remains an avid fan. For her, there is nothing like creating romantic stories and engaging plots, and each and every book is a new adventure. Cathy lives in London, and her three daughters—Charlotte, Olivia and Emma—have always been, and continue to be, the greatest inspirations in her life.

Books by Cathy Williams

Harlequin Presents

The Secret Sanchez Heir
Bought to Wear the Billionaire's Ring
Cipriani's Innocent Captive
Legacy of His Revenge
A Deal for Her Innocence
A Diamond Deal with Her Boss
The Tycoon's Ultimate Conquest
Contracted for the Spaniard's Heir
Marriage Bargain with His Innocent
The Italian's Christmas Proposition

Conveniently Wed!

Shock Marriage for the Powerful Spaniard

One Night With Consequences

The Italian's One-Night Consequence

Visit the Author Profile page
at Harlequin.com for more titles.

Cathy Williams

HIS SECRETARY'S NINE-MONTH NOTICE

HARLEQUIN
PRESENTS

If you purchased this book without a cover you should be aware
that this book is stolen property. It was reported as "unsold and
destroyed" to the publisher, and neither the author nor the
publisher has received any payment for this "stripped book."

HARLEQUIN®
PRESENTS®

Recycling programs
for this product may
not exist in your area.

ISBN-13: 978-1-335-14851-3

His Secretary's Nine-Month Notice

Copyright © 2020 by Cathy Williams

All rights reserved. No part of this book may be used or reproduced in
any manner whatsoever without written permission except in the case of
brief quotations embodied in critical articles and reviews.

This is a work of fiction. Names, characters, places and incidents
are either the product of the author's imagination or are used fictitiously.
Any resemblance to actual persons, living or dead, businesses,
companies, events or locales is entirely coincidental.

This edition published by arrangement with Harlequin Books S.A.

For questions and comments about the quality of this book,
please contact us at CustomerService@Harlequin.com.

Harlequin Enterprises ULC
22 Adelaide St. West, 40th Floor
Toronto, Ontario M5H 4E3, Canada
www.Harlequin.com

Printed in U.S.A.

HIS SECRETARY'S
NINE-MONTH NOTICE

To my three wonderful daughters,
Charlotte, Olivia and Emma

CHAPTER ONE

VIOLET'S FINGER HOVERED over the send button on her work email. She could already feel the emptiness of loss sinking its teeth into her and she breathed in deeply, banking down the rising panic at the thought of the unknown opening up at her feet like a gaping, bottomless hole. She wasn't a kid any more. She was a twenty-six-year-old adult. And being afraid of what lay around the corner was no longer appropriate. She could deal with this.

She clicked the button, closed her eyes and blanked out all the background noises of life happening outside her little mews house at seven thirty on a lovely summer Sunday evening in London.

She knew exactly how her boss was going to react to the email that would pop up on his laptop.

For starters—thank God—he wouldn't actually read it until the following morning, when he would breeze into the office at the usual ridiculously early time of six thirty. He would make himself a cup of strong black coffee, sit at his desk—which was always littered with papers, notes scribbled on sticky notes, reports and an impressive array of stationery, most of which he never used—and then he would start his day.

Top of the list would be reading his emails, and hers would be there, and he would open it, and he would… *hit the roof.*

She stood up and stretched, easing her aching joints. There was only so much she could focus on at any one point, she decided, and focusing on her boss and how he was going to react to her resignation would have to be put on hold. She would be facing him soon enough when she went into work the following day, later than usual at the far safer hour of nine thirty, when the place would be buzzing with people and there might just be less chance of him erupting in front of interested spectators.

Not that Matt Falconer ever seemed to give a hoot about what other people thought. He was a law unto himself. In the two-and-a-half years that she had worked for him, she had seen him storm out of high-level meetings because a lawyer, a CEO or a director had rubbed him the wrong way or, more often than not, failed to follow his outspoken and always brilliant logic. She had restrained him from slamming down incorrectly typed reports on the desk of whichever poor employee had submitted them. She had worked alongside him into the early hours of the morning to complete a deal because *it just can't wait.* She had tactfully made herself scarce when he had gone into a funk, staring at the four walls of his office, feet on his desk, hands folded behind his head, because inspiration had temporarily deserted him.

She had prepared herself a salad earlier, but her heart wasn't in it as she dug her fork into lettuce leaves, beetroot and all the other good stuff that invariably tasted like sawdust after five seconds.

Her head was too full.

In the space of just a week, her life had been turned on its head, and she was still reeling.

Violet didn't like change. She didn't care for surprises. She liked order, stability and...*routine*. She loved all the things other girls her age generally despised.

She didn't want adventure. She certainly would never have contemplated jacking in her job although, deep down, she knew that she would have had to sooner or later, because...over time, her feelings for her brilliant, temperamental, utterly unpredictable boss had become just a little too uncomfortable. But to be forced into giving it up...!

She pushed away her plate and stared around her, taking in her surroundings. She felt as though she was seeing them for the first time, but of course that made no sense, because she had been living here, in this beautiful little town house, since she had turned twenty. However, the prospect of renting it to a perfect stranger made her take stock of what she had. Years of perfectly positioned memorabilia...the bookcase heavy with the weight of her tomes of musical works, the manuscripts with so many notations made over the years, the pictures and ornaments and posters...

Tears threatened. Again.

She swallowed them back and turned her attention to tidying up the kitchen while the radio played in the background. Classical music, of course. Her favourite.

She only became aware of someone at the door by the banging, relentless and unnecessary, because whoever it was hadn't even had the common decency to give her time to get to the door.

She hurried out to pull it open before the neighbours started complaining...and there he was.

Matt Falconer. Her boss and the last person she'd expected to see standing on her doorstep. How on earth did the man even know where she lived?

She'd certainly never told him! She'd turned reticence about her private life into an art form.

Violet felt a guilty wash of colour flood her face. Caught on the back foot like this, without any time at all to brace herself for the impact he had on her, she could only stare at him, drinking in the stunningly beautiful lines of his lean face.

Two-and-a-half years and he still never failed to have this effect on her. He was so tall, so beautifully built, with wide shoulders, a tapered waist and long, muscular legs. His hair was just a little too long and his navy-blue eyes were fringed with the darkest, lushest of lashes. And, of course, there was his exotically bronze colouring; there had been Spanish blood on his mother's side somewhere along the line. Alongside him, other mere mortals always ended up looking wan, anaemic and pasty.

'What…? Er, s-sir, what are you doing here?' Violet stammered, tucking some straight, mousy-brown strands of hair behind her ear.

'Sir? *Sir?* Since when have I been knighted? Stand back. I want to come in!'

He straightened, and she automatically fell back, but her hand remained on the doorknob. The door was open a crack. One gentle push and she wouldn't stand a chance of keeping him out. And, from the thunderous look on his face, he wasn't going to think too hard about forcing an entry.

'It's Sunday,' Violet said, using her calm voice, the voice she saved for work, and specifically for her wildly temperamental boss. 'I expect you've come about my… er…letter… Well, email…'

'Letter? *Letter?*' Matt roared. 'A *letter* somehow implies that the contents are going to be *polite*!'

'You're going to disturb the neighbours,' Violet snapped.

'Then let me bloody come in and they won't be disturbed!'

'It was a very polite letter of resignation.'

'Want to have this conversation out here, Violet? I'm happy to knock on all the doors of your well-heeled neighbours and invite them outside to have a good old time earwigging. Everyone likes being outdoors in sunny weather, after all, and all the better if there's a cabaret going on.'

'You're impossible, Matt.'

'Well, at least we've dropped the *sir*. That's a start. Let me in. I need something strong to drink.'

He rested the flat of his hand on the door. Violet sighed and opened it, and then she stood to one side so that he could brush past her into the small but exquisite hall, with its black-and-white flagstones and rich colours.

For a few seconds, he said nothing. He just turned a full circle and stared, taking his time, looking at everything while she remained where she was, already predicting the questions he would ask and resenting the answers she would be forced to give.

When his gaze finally settled on her, there was lively curiosity alongside the raging anger that had brought him to her door.

'How did you get my address?' she asked.

'Going into the personnel files is hardly beyond the wit of man. Nice place, Violet. Who would have guessed?'

Violet reddened and glared at him. The infuriating man met her glare with a slow, curling smile, the smile of a shark that has suddenly and happily found itself sharing space with a tasty little morsel.

She spun round on her heels and headed straight for the kitchen.

The town house wasn't big, but neither was it small.

Off the hall, a highly polished staircase led up to the bedroom floor. Several doors opened out downstairs into a generous sitting room, a small snug that she used as her office and music room, a cloakroom lovingly displaying wallpaper and paint from its Victorian ancestry. And, of course, the kitchen, that was spacious enough to house a six-seater kitchen table on which were reams of papers that she hurriedly swept up into a bundle and dumped on the dresser. Then she turned to him, face still flaming red, leant against the counter and folded her arms.

Violet could not have felt more out of her comfort zone. Her neat work suits protected her from him, established all the necessary divisions between boss and secretary.

Here, in her house, dressed in a pair of jeans and an old tee shirt handed down from her dad's bad old days, she felt…exposed and horribly vulnerable.

But she wasn't going to let that show on her face.

'You never told me that you lived in an exquisite little jewel like this,' he mused, settling into one of the kitchen chairs, for all the world as though he was in it for the long haul.

'I don't believe I ever told you anything about where I lived,' Violet returned, and he tilted his head to one side and nodded slowly.

'My point exactly. Why would you hide this sort of thing from me? Most people keep quiet about their homes because they're embarrassed.'

'I have coffee,' Violet offered. 'Or tea. Which would you like?'

'Does that mean that there's no whisky lurking in any of the cupboards? No? Well, coffee it is, in that case. You know how I take it, Violet, because you know everything there is to know about me...'

He sank lower into the chair, his long body dwarfing it, his legs stretched out in front of him, his body language that of someone in no rush whatsoever. He folded his hands behind his head and looked at her with undisguised curiosity.

In terms of nightmares coming true, this was pretty much up there with the best of them.

Matt Falconer, billionaire legend of the IT and telecommunications world, the man adored by the press and women alike, in her house, nose twitching, because nothing would please him more than to ferret out information about her, information she had always made a point of keeping very firmly to herself.

From the very moment she had walked into his office, nestled high up in one of London's most iconic buildings, she had sensed that her boss wasn't going to be like the other two guys for whom she had worked. He wasn't going to be affable or fatherly like George Hill, with whom she had worked for two years before having been made redundant. Nor was he going to be anything like Simon Beesdale, her last boss, who had been a proud new daddy with photos of his family spread along his desk, keen to integrate her into his 'other family', as he called his team of fifteen people, always smiling, always encouraging.

No, Matt Falconer had kicked off proceedings by turning up late on day one, leaving her kicking her heels in his office, and from thereon in she had been tossed into the deep end and left to fend for herself. She'd had to rise to the challenge and learn fast on the spot. And she'd enjoyed every second of it. She'd loved the early mornings and the late nights, the buzz of activity and the frenetic, fast pace. She'd enjoyed the informality of the working environment, even though, orderly as she was, she knew she really shouldn't. And she'd kept up, earning his respect and seeing her salary rise several times in the space of two years.

But Matt's brilliant intellect and demanding work ethic were twined with staggering self-assurance of the kind she found vaguely disconcerting, an abundance of charm that brought out every cautious instinct in her and an inquisitive, questioning personality that was programmed to ignore all boundaries and every single do-not-trespass sign.

She had stood firm against the barrage of questions that had greeted her on a daily basis when she'd first joined his company. She had sidestepped the idle prying into her private life and had failed to rise to the bait when, in week three, he had told her with a certain amount of tetchiness in his voice that women tended to respond when he showed interest in their private lives.

'I'm afraid that won't be me,' she had murmured,

with a blatant lack of sincere apology in her voice. 'I believe in keeping my private life strictly separate from my working life.'

And she had not regretted her decision because, as time had moved on, as she had with deep reluctance fallen further and further under the spell of her charismatic boss, she could only thank the Lord that common sense had prevailed from the outset.

So his presence here now, in her charming mews house, was sending her body into panicked overdrive.

'For instance,' he was drawling now, 'I'm guessing that you know me well enough to have realised that I should have been out with Clarissa at the ballet this evening…and so wouldn't have read your email until tomorrow morning. Presumably, you intended to waltz in at some ungodly, late hour in the hope that I might have digested the bare bone message that you're walking out on the best paid job you could hope to find. Not to mention the most invigorating.'

Violet wiped her perspiring hands on her jeans and busied herself making his cup of coffee, just the way he liked it. Black, no sugar. With her back to him, she was spared the piercing intensity of those deep-blue eyes, but she could still feel them boring into her.

Like her, he was in casual clothes. Black jeans and a faded polo shirt and loafers. She'd seen him dressed down many times before. However, the fact that she was similarly dressed down was making her self-conscious and uncomfortable.

'That's not true,' she said, eyes downcast as she pushed a cup of coffee towards him and then took up position on the chair at the farthest end of the kitchen table.

She knew him well enough to know that his curiosity about her personal circumstances had not conveniently vanished into the ether. There just happened to be the more pressing matter of her resignation for him to contend with first, then he would return to the subject of where she lived.

She quailed with apprehension, but her smile remained composed, her expression polite and tolerant, if a little puzzled.

Just the sort of professional image she wanted to convey.

'So you *didn't* remember that I was supposed to be at the ballet...'

'Does it matter?'

'I'm disappointed in you, Violet. I thought we were friends and yet, here you are, too scared to tell me to my face that you're bailing on me.'

'I work for you, Matt, that's all,' she countered and he shook his head sadly.

'So do two hundred other employees who occupy the four storeys of that glass house, but none of them knows me as well as you do. Although...' He paused. 'If you'd known me well enough, you would have known that Clarissa and I were on the verge of breaking up. Going to the ballet with her was just one step too far.'

'You've broken up with her?' Violet felt a twinge of sympathy for the voluptuous, blond-haired, blue-eyed woman who might not be the sharpest knife in the block, but was bubbly, friendly and hardly deserving of the obligatory bunch of goodbye flowers that Violet would no doubt be asked to send in the next few days. If he didn't react to her resignation by showing her the door with immediate effect.

'Don't look so shocked,' Matt said drily. 'You know my life is too busy for committed long-term relation-ships. Anyway, we're going off-piste here. I came about that resignation email and I want to know why you've suddenly decided, out of the blue, that you're fed up working for me. Is it the money? If it is, then you could simply have approached me and made your case for a pay rise.'

Violet was momentarily distracted by her boss's sweeping assumption that any relationship longer than five seconds qualified as *committed* and *long-term*.

She blinked and focused on him. Her heart sped up and her pulse raced as their eyes tangled, deep-blue meeting guarded brown. She knew that she was blush-ing and she hated herself for not having the wherewithal to maintain an air of indifference and neutrality. At work, in her neat suit—grey jacket, white shirt, grey skirt, sensible black pumps—she was well protected from the lethal impact of his charm, but she wasn't in her neat suit here.

Nor was her brain playing ball. She should have re-

membered that someone like Matt, who was God's gift
to the opposite sex, went for a certain type of woman.
Leggy, big-breasted, very, very blonde and with a line
in conversation that always included the phrases 'of
course', 'sure' and 'whatever you want'. He definitely
didn't go for little five-foot-three sparrows with straight
brown bobs, unremarkable features and slender, flat-
chested bodies who stood their ground whatever the
provocation.

Why on earth had he descended on her like this?
What gave him the right? It was unfair that he should
be sitting in her kitchen, lounging back in one of her
chairs and getting under her skin when she already had
so much on her plate!

'Of course it's not the money,' she said, swallow-
ing some of her coffee and wincing because it was so
hot. 'And, yes, if I was unsatisfied with my pay then
I wouldn't resign, Matt. I would approach you to discuss it.'

'So, if not the money, what then?' he demanded
forcefully. 'You can't say that the job lacks challenge.
Hell, Violet, you've got more responsibility than any of
the women who have ever worked for me in the past.'

'That's because none of them have stayed very long.'

'Rubbish.' He waved aside that riposte with a casual,
dismissive gesture, keeping his eyes very firmly fixed
on her face. 'Admittedly, a number of them were short-
lived, but none of them had what it took to cope with
anything but the lightest of workloads.'

Violet lowered her eyes and said nothing. When she'd joined, the personnel manager had been tearing his hair out.

'It's a difficult situation.' He had all but groaned with frustration. 'Matt is very...er...demanding... Lots of past candidates have found him impossible to work for. They've also mentioned that he makes them nervous. They're perfectly capable when they enter the building, and they've all passed the series of interviews with flying colours, but ten minutes with him and their nerves are shredded...'

She'd understood exactly what he'd meant the minute she'd spent five minutes in his company. Matt Falconer was brutally clever, horribly intolerant if you couldn't keep up and so spectacularly good-looking that it was a wonder *anyone* had been able to work for him for longer than a day without having their brains scrambled.

Thankfully, she was made of sterner stuff. Life had prepared her for just about anything, and she had dealt with her boss the way she had dealt with all the larger-than-life, crazily impulsive and wildly unpredictable people who had entered and left her life, thanks to her father. With equanimity, keeping to herself and protecting herself behind a wall of impenetrable calm.

'If you want more responsibility,' he growled, 'then say so. I can give you a title...more work...varied projects. You name it.'

'It's not the work.'

'Then what the hell is it?' He narrowed his eyes and

sat forward, resting his elbows on his thighs and staring at her until she wanted to squirm with discomfort. 'Has someone been making life difficult for you?'

'What are you talking about?' Violet looked at him with genuine bewilderment.

'Some of those guys who work with me can be a little overboisterous. Comes with the territory, I'm afraid. Working on computer apps and dealing with innovative start-up companies requires a different kind of personality to the stuffy sort who work in banks and insurance companies. There's a chance you might be finding one of them impossible to deal with. Is that it? Give me a name and they get the sack. Instantly. Wait.'

He paused and Violet was too confused by this sudden tangent to say anything. 'Clients have been coming and going for the past few weeks with that new takeover. You know the one I mean… Food-app developer I'm in the process of buying out… Has one of them been pestering you? Is that it? I've noticed that that Draper boy has been lurking by your desk…'

'Matt, I know how to take care of myself!' Two bright patches of colour stained her cheeks.

How pathetic did he think she was? So pathetic that she would resign from a job she loved because someone decided to chat her up?

Suddenly, she was so angry that she wanted to slap him, so she balled her small hands into fists and counted to ten.

She could feel the tension of the past few days simmering, boiling up, spilling over, and she had to bite down on the temptation to shout at him. She wasn't the shouting sort. For a second, she wondered how he would react if his perennially unflappable PA decided to let rip.

'Do you?' he was asking quietly. 'You're quiet, Violet. Refined. Not the sort to give as good as she gets.'

'I wish you could hear yourself, Matt Falconer,' Violet responded, heading fast towards a flashpoint and only holding off by sheer willpower. 'I'm not a complete idiot.'

He had the grace to flush. 'I never said that you were.'

'The implication was there,' Violet retorted scornfully, and she noted the startled expression on his face, because this was a side to her he hadn't seen. 'You think I'm such a weak fool that if someone says "boo", then I'm going to go crying and running away because I just can't handle it!'

'Not at all,' he muttered uncomfortably.

'I'll have you know that I have a great deal more backbone than you probably think!'

'I'm sure you have.'

'Then stop patronising me!'

'Jesus, Violet. Where is this coming from? I only came here to find out what was going on!' He raked his fingers through his hair and Violet gathered herself, but with difficulty.

'I've handed in my notice, Matt, because something has cropped up, something unexpected, and I haven't had a choice.' She took a deep breath. 'I know that my email was a bit...er...brief, but going into details would have been complicated. I had no idea you would pursue the matter.'

'You thought that I would just sit back and let you walk out on me?' Matt demanded incredulously, and Violet blushed, because the phrasing of those words was so unintentionally intimate.

Good job you're leaving! She mentally berated herself for all her negative thoughts involving voids opening up at the prospect of never going into that fast-paced, adrenaline-charged office ever again. *Just remember how dangerous it is, having a stupid crush on your boss!*

'I'll make sure I find a suitable replacement before I leave,' she responded coolly. 'I won't leave you in the lurch.'

'What if I decide that you're irreplaceable?'

Violet shrugged. She wished he would tailor his remarks, which were just making her even more addled and flustered, but naturally he wouldn't because Matt Falconer never saw fit to tailor his words or his actions to suit anyone. He was a law unto himself. That was just how he liked it and, annoyingly, he got away with it because he was so over-the-top talented at what he did.

'No one's irreplaceable.'

'You say that you didn't have a choice,' he thought aloud, his expression clearing. He sat forward so abruptly that she blinked in sudden confusion. 'You're pregnant, aren't you? I'm very progressive when it comes to things like that, but is he a dinosaur? Is that it? Someone with a value system that's still buried in the Middle Ages? It would be a travesty for some guy to think that a pregnant woman equates to a stay-at-home partner.'

Deep-blue eyes darted down to her stomach and, horrified, Violet instinctively rested her hand on her tummy. 'Who is he, Violet, and how is it that I don't know a thing about him? Isn't that taking secrecy to the very limit?' He shot her an accusatory look from under thick, sooty lashes. 'And tell me that you're enough of a feminist to know that you don't jack a great job in because some guy with antiquated expectations suggests that you do.'

Suddenly restless, he vaulted upright and walked in jerky movements to the kitchen window, staring out for a few seconds before spinning round to glare at her, clearly offended.

'We no longer live in the Dark Ages,' he carried on, leaving her speechless at his wild conclusions. 'And you should know that I am more than considerate when it comes to taking care of my staff, including the ones who have babies. Is there or is there not a crèche available, expertly manned by fully trained staff, on the eighth floor?'

'Yes, but...'

'We've long left behind those bad old days of gender inequality.'

'There's nothing wrong with being a stay-at-home mum!' Violet was distracted enough to retort.

Frankly, she could think of nothing more wonderful, but she wasn't going to become diverted by this non-issue. How on earth could someone with such an incredibly sharp brain be so...*dense*?

'You're not wearing a ring,' he commented sharply. 'Baby out of wedlock, Violet? Not what I would have expected, but then it's very obvious that you've been keeping all sorts of things from me. I'm beginning to wonder whether I knew you at all! Naturally, you never gave anything away, but I thought I knew the kind of person you were. Hasn't the man had the decency to propose to you, or has he done a runner?'

He shook his head in disgust while Violet did her best to keep up, even though her brain was lagging several light years behind. 'Or maybe he's married. Is that it? Did you get yourself embroiled in some kind of sordid situation that's ended up leading to this? You should have come to me for advice, Violet. I would have been there for you.'

Violet stared at him with undisguised incredulity. She was so astounded that she could barely think straight.

'A married man? A sordid affair? And, Matt Falconer, not that it has ever been necessary, but why on earth would I ever contemplate coming to you for advice?'

Matt frowned. 'Because I'm a man of the world,' he

said in a voice that implied that he was doing nothing more than stating the obvious.

'You're also a man who has never had a relationship that's lasted longer than three months!' she was riled into retorting, betraying her code of never losing her cool with her boss. Naturally, instead of being annoyed with her outburst, he stared at her with the expression of a man suddenly intrigued.

She had half risen from her chair through sheer frustration, and now he slowly strolled towards her.

Mesmerised against her will, Violet could only stare right back at him as he drew closer until he was standing right in front of her, at which point she sank back into the chair, trembling all over and angry with herself for letting the situation get so completely out of hand.

'This is ridiculous!' she exclaimed, watching warily as he dragged a chair across so that he was sitting far too close to her for comfort's sake.

'I know. It is. So why don't you just take back your resignation and we'll pretend none of this ever happened?' He looked at her narrowly and suddenly, inexplicably, found his imagination start to wander because there was something oddly fetching about her flushed face, parted lips and angry eyes. He frowned and blinked away that sudden drag on his senses.

'I haven't resigned because I want a pay rise.' She tabulated each point carefully and slowly. 'Nor is it because I want more responsibility. If you had read what I said in my email, you'd have noted that I was extremely complimentary about my experience of working for your company—'

'You sound like a cheap brochure when you say that,' Matt interrupted.

Violet bristled. Not only had he interrupted, but he was so damned close that his knees were touching hers and it was hellishly impossible to focus properly.

'Nor,' she continued through gritted teeth, 'has anyone been pestering me on the work front, and if John Draper happened to ask me out on a date, then that is none of your business!'

'I knew that guy was lurking round your desk for no good reason.' Matt scowled and Violet wanted to hit him.

'And more to the point, Matt Falconer, I have *not* been having an affair with anyone! I am *not* pregnant and I certainly could never be attracted to anyone who thought that it might be okay to lay down ground rules about a woman's place. That is not why I have had to tender my resignation!'

'That's good.' He was visibly relieved by that assertion and Violet glared at him. He was just so selfish, she thought waspishly. All he cared about was whether he could get a saint who would be able to cope with his unpredictable, demanding personality! She couldn't believe that she had actually been idiotic enough to have fallen for the guy! Thank God she was savvy enough to know how to contain her inappropriate reaction. Thank

God lusting from afar was a curable sickness, and cured she would be as soon as she left his employ.

'So, tell me what this nonsense is all about.' He relaxed back and gazed at her, and she just couldn't help drinking in his insane good looks, at least for a second, until she blinked herself back to reality.

She sighed and surrendered.

CHAPTER TWO

'IT'S MY FATHER,' she said quietly, and he stared at her as though she had suddenly started speaking in tongues.

'You have a father?'

'Yes, Matt. I have a father. People do. These things happen.'

He grinned and shifted, angling his chair so that he could stretch his legs out in front of him. 'I would say that I would miss your sarcasm, but I won't, because if this is a simple case of parental problems then I'm sure we'll be able to work around it.'

'I'm not sarcastic,' Violet told him politely, and his eyebrows shot up.

'You've made more sarcastic remarks about the women I date than I've had hot dinners.'

Had she? She'd always thought that she was scrupulously non-committal when it came to the blondes who entered and left his life through an ever-revolving door.

'Remember asking me if I'd ever thought of dating women who didn't get worked up about going on spa breaks? Or the time you said that it wasn't true that blondes had more fun? And let's not forget some of your unnecessary asides about my tokens of affection when a relationship has, sadly, run its course…'

'Tokens of affection?' Violet retorted. 'I honestly don't think that expensive bouquets of flowers from the same expensive flower shop in Knightsbridge could be called "tokens of affection."'

'I've given far more than flowers in the past.'

'When it comes to a break-up, there's no such thing as a token of affection.'

'Which, anyway, is just my arrogant way of appeasing my conscience.'

'You said it,' Violet muttered. 'I didn't.'

'Actually, you did,' Matt returned without batting an eyelid. 'More than once although, admittedly, in various guises. Same message, however. Most people think twice when it comes to letting their opinions go into free fall when they're with me, but you have never been reticent when it comes to saying what you think about my personal life. In your own quiet way, of course. So what's the problem with your father?'

Violet could feel her skin burning. Had she really been that obvious? Or had the man noticed and retained every small, passing, barely audible remark she had made about some of his life choices? She thought she'd always been so careful, but clearly she hadn't been nearly as careful as that.

'I… My father…isn't well…'

'I'm sorry to hear that, Violet. Serious? How old is he?'

There was genuine sympathy in his voice, and something inside her weakened. She wasn't accustomed to sharing, but right now she wanted nothing more than to spill her heart out to the man sitting opposite her with his head tilted to one side, his deep-blue eyes speculative and thoughtful.

'How old is he?' she repeated briskly. 'Young. Not yet sixty.'

'What's wrong with him?'

'It's not really relevant, Matt.' Violet shrugged, ignoring the temptation to say more than she knew she should. Her privacy was so important to her, so much an ingrained trait, that it was almost impossible to shed even when she wanted to.

It was a habit born from circumstance. Life on the move had put paid to friendships. How easy was it ever to formulate firm bonds with people you met in passing? Especially when you were young, too young to think ahead to the bigger picture. And of course, by the time life had become more settled, that habit had taken root, and those roots ran very deep indeed.

'Of course it's relevant,' he said quietly. 'You're upset.'

'And you're imagining things.'

'You don't have to put on a brave front all the time,' was his response, and she bristled, not liking the way he seemed to be circling her, making her feel lost and vulnerable. 'Talk to me. You've handed in your notice. I think it's fair to say that I deserve more of an explanation than "thank you for the opportunity to work for you. I've enjoyed my experience at your company, however, I feel that it's time to move on…"'

Of course he did. Violet realised that somewhere, deep down, she would have been disappointed if he had accepted her letter of resignation with a philosophical shrug of those broad shoulders, no questions asked.

She'd worked for him and alongside him for two-and-a-half years and, yes, she had gradually come to see she knew him in ways far deeper than any of the women he went out with. She knew his idiosyncrasies, his quirks. And he, it would appear, knew her far better than she had ever imagined. It was unsettling, to say the least.

Besides, nothing he could say would change her decision, so where was the harm in a little confiding? She would leave his company and leave him behind and, if he had glimpsed that private side to her, then it wasn't as if afterwards she would be facing him day after day, having to deal with his renewed curiosity in some awful *Groundhog Day* loop.

'My father lives on the other side of the world,' she began, frowning, getting her thoughts in order. 'Australia, to be precise.'

'How long as he been there? Where in Australia?'

'Melbourne. He's been there for…nearly six years. He went after… Well, he remarried. My mother died when I was young.' She chewed her lip and looked away and Matt didn't say anything. He hated crying women. Just something else she knew about him—and she did

her utmost to make sure she didn't give in to the wave
of maudlin despondency threatening to ambush all her
good intentions.

'Take your time. I'm in no hurry.'

'Sure you want this kind of conversation?' Violet
lightened her tone, but when their eyes met there was
no responding teasing in his. He looked deadly serious.

'Why wouldn't I?'

'Because you don't do long, intense conversations
with women. I think that's something you've shared
with me in the past.'

'How well you know me,' Matt murmured, with a
certain amount of amusement. 'You're not one of my
women, though, are you? So it's fair to say that normal
rules of engagement don't apply.'

Not one of his women…

Violet felt a sharp pang somewhere deep inside her,
a sharp and utterly inappropriate pang. Thank good-
ness she *wasn't* 'one of his women,' she told herself.
Knowing him as well as she did, that would have been
a recipe for heartbreak, because he represented everything she didn't want in a guy and would never want.

She might have been a sucker for those sinful, dark
looks—who wouldn't be?—but she was way too sensible
to go any further down that dangerous road of attraction.

She shrugged, expression veiled. To kill time and
get her thoughts in order, she offered him a top up on
the coffee and, when he politely declined, she reluc-

tantly suggested a glass of wine, which he accepted with alacrity.

'So, you were telling me about your father…the one you've avoided mentioning for the past two-and-a-half years…who lives in Melbourne, a place I know well.'

'He's had problems with his liver, which he's coped with well enough, but my stepmother died six months ago, and ever since then he's been getting more and more depressed,' Violet said abruptly. She needed a bit of wine as well, and she poured herself a glass before sitting back down. 'He visited for two weeks a couple of months ago and he tried to put a brave face on things, but I could see through that.'

'Liver problems… Drinker?'

Violet reddened. Of course, he would ask questions.

'He used to be, but as you know, drink is always the devil waiting in the wings when it comes to ex…ex…'

'Alcoholics?'

She nodded brusquely and looked away. 'Depression is his enemy and I'm very much afraid that, left to his own devices, he may find that devil on his shoulder just a little bit too tempting.'

'He's still in Melbourne?'

'Yes.'

'Why doesn't he move back over here?' Matt looked around the bijou mews house and Violet could see what he was thinking without him having to spell it out.

The house might not be a mansion, but it was big enough for two. It was certainly worth a lot of money

and could easily be sold and something bigger purchased in a less flashy postcode.

'Money issues?'

'If there were money issues I wouldn't be living in
a place like this.'

'Which brings me to the question I've been meaning to ask since I walked through your front door...'
He paused for a heartbeat, then continued with more
urgency in his voice. 'I don't give a damn how you're
managing to afford the rent on a place like this. Maybe
you have a thing for small, expensive houses and would
rather sacrifice your monthly pay cheque renting one
of them than throwing your hard-earned cash away on
holidays, fast cars and designer clothes. Your business.
Bottom line is, if you can't afford to support your father
if he returns here, then say the word.'

'Holidays, fast cars and designer clothes?' Violet
parroted faintly, wondering if he was actually talking
about *her*.

'You know where I'm going with this. If it's money
you're after, then I'm prepared to throw as much as you
need your way. We can call it a loan with zero interest
rate.' He raked his fingers through his hair and stared
at her. 'I never thought I'd beg for any woman.' He shot
her a crooked smile that did all the wrong things to her
nervous system. 'But I'm big enough to concede that
there's always a first time for everything.' This time
his expression was serious. 'No one has ever worked

so well with me before. You understand how I think and you don't go into a tailspin if I get too close to you.'

Violet knew that there was a huge compliment in there somewhere, but all she could think about was *you don't go into a tailspin if I get too close to you.* He could say that with certainty because the unspoken rider was that they both knew he could never find her attractive, so why would she be affected by him the way other, more suitably blonde and busty women might be?

Gossip over the years had informed her that the only PA who had ever stuck it out with him—and she had stuck it out for a lifetime—had been a sixty-year-old married grandmother who had taken early retirement, leaving him in the lurch three years previously. Before Violet had come along, the vacant spot had been filled by an unsatisfactory procession of attractive potentials because, one of the girls in Accounts had confided after a couple of after-work drinks, he'd decided he liked a bit of eye candy.

'Not very PC,' Violet had responded, and Amelia had burst out laughing.

'Oh, Matt wouldn't even be aware of it! No, that's just the conclusion we all reached after a while. Problem is, he's a hunk, and girls go into a tizzy when he's around. Even bigger problem is that he really doesn't get it. Which is why he's kept making the same mistake over and over.'

Until me, Violet had thought.

'I'm very flattered,' she said now, banking down all

negative thoughts about her appearance. 'But it's nothing to do with the money.'

Violet sighed and resigned herself to the fact that he would be shocked at a past she had always kept to herself. She stood up, opened one of the drawers and pulled out a photo album, which she handed to him, because in this case, pictures would speak so much more clearly than words.

He opened it. Flicked through the pages. Sat up just a little bit straighter and flicked through the pages again, more slowly, inspecting each and every one. Then he looked at her with astonishment.

'Your father is *Mickey Dunn*?'

'Real name Victor. I'm surprised you've heard of him.'

'Who hasn't? Burnt out young. Drink and drugs.'

'Stop looking at me like that,' Violet said irritably. She drained her glass and felt the buzz of alcohol race to her head. She barely drank. A legacy from being around people who did very little *but*.

'I would never have guessed that you were the daughter of a hellraiser like Mickey Dunn,' Matt murmured, unashamedly curious. He glanced round the kitchen as though seeing it for the first time. 'That explains this place,' he said slowly. 'And all the while, I thought you were saving hard to buy somewhere, being careful with what you earned, avoiding holidays like the plague because a mortgage was more important. And then I figured you were renting. Presumably, you own the place lock, stock and smoking barrels?'

'I never lied to you,' Violet said defensively, and he just looked at her with the sort of shuttered expression that made her feel as though she had, somehow, deliberately deceived him, which of course she *hadn't*.

'You're right,' he said, in a voice as smooth as silk. There was a coldness there that went to the very core of her, making her realise how used to his teasing she had become, to the warmth of those fabulous deep-blue eyes, to the respect that was always there whenever he addressed her.

Things she had taken for granted and, although it hardly mattered now what he thought of her, it was just too painful not to try to justify herself, to set the record straight, even though there was no need.

'My father bought this place for me before he left for Australia. He didn't like to think that I might be staying anywhere…dangerous. I always made it clear that I didn't want any money from him but he dug his heels in.' She smiled. 'You'd think he would have been a lot more relaxed about stuff like that, considering his misspent youth, but he wasn't.'

She took a deep breath and looked him straight in the eyes. 'My mum died when I was eight. In a motorcycle accident. My dad was driving and he never really recovered from the fact that she was pillion, even though he hadn't been drinking. Just skidded. Wet night… Took a corner too fast.'

'Where were you at the time?'

'At home. Home was a hotel room in… I can't even remember which country. Abroad. Paid babysitter. They partied hard but, when mum was alive, weirdly not as often as you'd think. Sometimes they took me but usually they were good at making sure that someone responsible was looking after me. I remember I woke up in the morning and nothing was the same after that. Anyway, to cut a long story short, the life of a rock star made him go off the rails completely. He lost himself in drink and drugs, even though he carried on doing his best for me. It was just that sometimes his best was a little…erratic.' She felt the tears welling up but she didn't dare make eye contact with her boss, just in case.

'He played music, and had his adoring fans, and we travelled the world, but I saw him when he was on his own. I saw the sadness. Eventually, of course, the band stopped touring, and for a while my dad wrote music for other people. By then, he was in and out of rehab and I had long become his carer. Of sorts.'

'His carer…'

'These things happen.' She shrugged. Thankfully, that moment of wanting to burst into tears had gone, and she was back in control now. The past was the past and she had come to terms with it a long time ago. She might not have had a normal childhood, but it had been colourful, and whatever the distractions, her dad had always been there for her. In his own way.

'So…' She began the process of winding up the con-

versation. She had said far more than she had anticipated and was thinking that it was just as well that their
time together was numbered. Matt Falconer recognised
no boundaries when it came to digging deep, and her
story would have stoked his curiosity, no doubt about
that. His spade would be at the ready, and she quailed
at the thought of what her life would have been like if
she'd carried on working for him indefinitely.

'My plan is to rent this place out and go to Australia
for a while to be with my dad. He doesn't want to return
to London to live. He enjoys Melbourne and he's made
friends over there. He likes the weather and the laid-
back lifestyle. But I need to make sure that he's okay
while he goes through this temporary blip.'

She waited for him to say something, but he was
worryingly silent.

'It would have been different if Caroline, my stepmother, was still around.'

Silence.

'He's on the waiting list for a liver transplant, if you
must know.'

Way too much confiding, Violet thought, angry with
herself.

'He met her when he was in rehab. She was a mem-
ber of staff there.'

She clicked her tongue impatiently and wondered
whether she would just keep babbling into the silence
until every thought she had and every feeling she'd ever
felt had been laid bare. This wasn't like her at all. This

wasn't the cool, private, detached Violet Dunn he was accustomed to.

'Are you just going to sit there, Matt?' she found herself compelled to snap.

'You were his carer…' Matt repeated, still pensive and still staring at her in the sort of intense, focused way that made the hairs at the back of her neck stand on end. 'Something must have been sacrificed.'

'What do you mean?'

'The way it usually works,' he said slowly, as if piecing together a complex problem that could only be solved through a series of careful stages, 'is the carer gives something up. Am I right? I'm guessing your education would have been erratic, to say the least, which incidentally says a lot about the fact that you still managed to attain so many qualifications. You must have burnt the midnight oil as a teenager.'

Violet's mouth tightened. If only he knew the extent of the role reversal that had characterised her life! She had not really given it a second thought, growing up, but she had often looked back over the years and gazed at the adolescent who had stayed at home, head in a book, while her dad had been out getting drunk, doing drugs and staggering back in to flop in a heap on the sofa. She had been the one admonishing him about late nights and preaching about the dangers of drugs. She had made sure he took his vitamins and had his five a day whenever possible. By the time the touring had come to an end and the rehab visits had started, she had been very much used to running the household.

So had she given things up?

Had she ever! And top of the list was the carefree, reckless joy of adolescence.

'I enjoyed studying,' she said vaguely. 'It's time you left. You asked me to explain why I had to resign and I have.'

'I'm not ready to go.'

'What do you mean, you're *not ready to go*?'

'I've spent two-and-a-half years wondering what made my überefficient secretary tick…' He leant back in the chair and looked at her from under lowered lashes. 'You'll have to excuse my curiosity. Also, I'm still in the game of trying to get you to change your mind. Likewise, you'll have to excuse my persistence.'

'Can we talk about this in the morning?' she asked wearily.

'You mean when you're in your prim little suit, sitting behind your desk with your professional hat firmly flattened on your head? I think I prefer this slightly less formal Violet Dunn.'

'I don't care what you prefer!'

'I've just taken on two start-up software companies and one of them happens to be in Melbourne. Small start-up in the city. Did you know Melbourne is right up there when it comes to density of small businesses? Getting a foothold there is a coup for me. Lots of promise there and I'm going to nurture this baby. I feel this goose might lay a few golden eggs with the right backing, expertise and encouragement.'

'What does this have to do with me?' Violet queried, standing up and hovering when he didn't automatically follow suit. She dimly recalled those two companies, because the very young directors in search of investment had been brought over to discuss details, and they had been full of it.

She walked to the kitchen door and rested her hand lightly on the doorknob.

'You need routine,' Matt said in a soothing voice that made her grit her teeth together in exasperation. How was it that he could manage to make something as laudable as needing routine sound like a dismal admission of failure?

'I think my life will carry on without it for a while,' Violet responded tartly. 'Get up. It's time to go. I'm exhausted.'

'So I take it that you're not planning on settling down on the other side of the world?'

Violet clicked her tongue and refused to give him the satisfaction of sitting back down, even though he was making less than zero effort to take the hint and leave.

'No,' she conceded after a while. She sighed and sat back down. This wasn't a victory for him, she reasoned, but plain old common sense from her because if he wanted to carry on talking for ten more minutes, then he wasn't going to budge, and her legs were feeling distinctly wobbly—probably because she had had her personal space invaded. 'I couldn't live over there. It would be a lot easier for Dad to move back here, and that's going to be part of my job when I go over. To convince him to return to London.'

'If he's still got ties here, he might think that they could lead him astray,' Matt suggested shrewdly, and Violet's eyes widened.

'I never thought of that,' she admitted slowly. 'You could be right. He's still pals with the members in his band, and of course they still go to the pub and drink, which would be tough for him. I could persuade him to move closer to the coast. Far enough from London for temptation not to be right there on his doorstep...' She looked at Matt and realised that this was just another of his talents—an ability to see through the clutter and chaos and get right to the heart of the problem in record time.

She had absorbed that trait, just as she had absorbed all those others, and now she wondered whether, subconsciously, they had all bonded together to turn professional respect for him into something altogether more dangerous.

'But back to this little start-up of mine,' Matt drawled, and Violet blinked and focused on him, her mind still playing with the disturbing realisation that he had managed to crawl under her skin a lot more than she had ever suspected.

'The reason I mention it,' he continued with a gesture that smacked ever so slightly of a certain smug satisfaction, 'is because I could use a safe pair of hands over there—steering the newly acquired ship, so to speak. On every single front, it would work for both of us.'

'What do you mean?'

'I mean, Violet, that you plan on disappearing for months—and having nothing to do on the other side of the world except rally your father's spirits is going to get very frustrating for you after a very, very short while. You have a good brain and you need to use it. How are you going to do that in Melbourne? Maybe find some casual work behind a bar somewhere? Or else you could take up a hobby. Something you could make use of within the confines of the four walls of your father's house so that you can keep a watchful eye on him.'

'Stop being so negative.' Violet looked at him steadily and calmly. There had been enough departures from common sense for the evening, thank you very much. 'I'm sure I'll be able to occupy myself when I'm out there.'

'Yes, there'll be adequate cash-in-hand casual labour jobs, although you obviously don't need the money, which will make any not-much-of-anything temp job all the more frustrating. And, of course, anything more challenging might prove a problem, as you're not a national. I've always got the impression that you enjoy a challenge.

'So, joining the dots here, you're going to be bored rigid…and I could use someone I trust implicitly in the initial stages of getting my new company in order. It'll be a sizeable promotion for you. In charge of one of my fledging companies from ground zero. New title, new set of responsibilities and, of course, new pay cheque to reflect both those things. Don't worry about work permits and all that tedious stuff. Consider it sorted.'

He allowed a few seconds to elapse so that she could digest all the considerable advantages to what he was offering.

And, Violet was forced to concede, they were indeed sizeable.

Boredom would weigh heavily on her hands. Yes, of course, her time would be devoted to her father, to raising his spirits and going with him for the medical check-ups that she'd recently discovered he had been ignoring. Lord only knew what else would be unearthed once she got over there. But how well this man knew her. How well he knew that doing nothing would get to her very quickly. However, there was one missing link not even Matt Falconer could factor in, and Violet had no intention of enlightening him.

'I could even set you up in a little apartment of your own, so that you and your father could maintain that very vital independence you've probably both grown accustomed to over the years, if you feel the need to bang the drum for financial independence. You could call it a perk that comes with the job.'

'That's a very generous offer, Matt…'

'So shall we call it a deal? Shake on it?' He dealt her one of those smiles that could knock a person for six.

'Of course, there would be one or two contingents you would have to take into consideration…'

'Of course there would be,' Violet said drily. 'There's no such thing as a free lunch. Isn't that written somewhere in your company manual?'

Matt burst out laughing and his eyes darkened with appreciation at the way she never had any qualms when it came to telling it like it was. Jesus, he would miss that!

'You would have to sign up to returning to my employ in London after a predetermined length of time, and I'd say that six months would be a pretty generous timescale. You might also have to put up with me descending on you intermittently, just to make sure that everything is ticking over nicely.'

'I'm very grateful for the offer, Matt.' Violet pictured him meeting her father and finding a foothold in her life in Melbourne and she suppressed a shudder. He had enough of an effect on her, and that was without him knowing a thing about her. 'But I'm going to have to say no.'

Matt carried on smiling for a few seconds, then he frowned as her words sank in. 'You don't mean that.'

'This situation has all been very sudden,' she said truthfully, 'but it's going to provide me with a break to explore other avenues aside from working behind a desk in an office.'

'What other avenues?'

'I know it's in my contract to work out my full six-week notice period, but if I find a replacement before then, would you consider freeing me of that obligation earlier? Naturally, I wouldn't be paid for any time I didn't work. Maybe you could sleep on that and we can discuss it when I come in tomorrow morning?'

'I can't believe I'm hearing this!'

She'd gone to the door and now he joined her, scowling.

'You don't always get what you want,' Violet told him gently.

'If you want to leave that desperately, then far be it from me to chain you to your desk and force you to work out your notice period!'

'You mean that? Because, the sooner I can be with my dad, the better.' He was going to release her from her contract, she thought. He'd done what for him was the equivalent of begging, and now he intended to throw the towel in the ring with his usual flamboyance. All or nothing. That was his nature.

It was terrifying.

But she kept smiling as he stared down at her, glowering. Then, quite unexpectedly, he rested his hand on the door to the sitting room, which was ajar, and half stumbled as it flew open. And there he was, in the sanctuary of her sitting room.

For a few seconds, he was lost for words as he stared at the baby grand piano positioned by the bay window. Violet followed his gaze. Without thinking, she walked towards the piano and gently smoothed her hand over the rich chestnut lid, then along the ivory-and-black keys, hardly aware of the picture she was painting, just doing something that was purely instinctive.

'You play?' Matt was mesmerised by just how slender and elegant a figure she cut, standing there, half-turned away from him, ethereal and wistful, exerting some weird magnetism over him.

He was right behind her. Violet could feel his warmth radiating outwards, swirling around her, but she didn't feel uncomfortable or self-conscious because this was her comfort zone. She absently played a few keys and a soft, melodious tune took shape under her moving fingers, then she stopped and turned to him, embarrassed now.

'I play,' she murmured. 'I must have inherited some of my father's musical talent.'

He was staring down at her with a veiled, oddly disturbing expression and she smiled, eager to lighten the moment and bring things back down to earth.

'Don't look so surprised, Matt. So what if I'm more than just the efficient, invisible secretary you've spent the past two-and-a-half years taking for granted?'

'Take you for granted? Never,' Matt murmured. His eyes drifted away from hers, down to the surprisingly full and perfectly shaped mouth. A *sexy* mouth, he realised, a mouth fashioned for kissing. 'Invisible? Hardly.'

The atmosphere had changed. Violet felt the shift and backed away, bumping into the piano and instantly straightening so that she didn't sit on the keys. He was so close to her and he was no longer her boss. They were man and woman, eyes locked, breathing laboured, suffused in an electric charge that was suddenly so potent that she wanted to pass out.

'You should go now,' she said huskily. For a few seconds he didn't move, and she wondered what she would do if the unthinkable happened—if that cool, firm, sensuous mouth covered hers.

He backed off, and when there was some safe distance between them he said, gruffly, 'One week. After that, Violet, you're free to go.' He spun round on his heels and headed for the door.

He was already opening the front door by the time she caught up with him. Her body was still burning, as though she'd stepped too close to a conflagration that had suddenly changed direction and begun soaring towards her at speed.

'What about me finding a replacement for you?' she asked, and he looked at her coolly.

'I'll manage.' He paused then said, cutting her to the quick, 'I thought I knew you, Violet. Turns out I couldn't be further from the truth.'

CHAPTER THREE

VIOLET WENT TO work the following morning, at the safe time of nine on the dot, to find the usually buzzing office almost completely empty.

'Hush-hush, top-secret meeting.' Lisa, one of the junior computer software analysts, approached her from behind and Violet spun round with a frown.

'Top-secret meeting? I didn't know that there were any meetings booked for today.' She peered in the direction of the conference room, but the door was open and there was no one inside.

'They've disappeared to one of the hotels. All the CEOs and the head of Accounts and a handful of the tech guys.' She began heading towards her desk and threw over her shoulder, 'Hey, you should be glad you've been spared that ordeal. You know how long they can go on for! Anyway, I'm holding the fort until they decide to start drifting back. Probably lunchtime. Knowing that lot from the tech team, they won't be passing up the subsidised meal in the office cafeteria.'

Bemused, Violet headed towards her office.

By the time she got there, it had sunk in that Matt had delivered what could only be called a body blow.

She had never been left out of anything. She had always been his right-hand woman, had sat in on all meetings. Very soon after she'd joined, he'd told her to scrap the boring business of taking minutes.

'I don't need you to remember on my behalf,' he had drawled in that self-assured way of his. 'I have an excellent memory. And so have you. Between the pair of us, we can remember what goes on in a two-hour meeting. Just make sure you transcribe as soon as we get back to the office.'

Now, here she was, twiddling her thumbs, ostensibly dumped from whatever high-level conference they had gone to.

Coding on new apps as they came to fruition, and before the process of launching them onto the market began, was often a game of timing and secrecy. Beating the competition was everything, and that rested on no one finding out what was going on within the hallowed walls of Matt's considerable business. Loyalty was of the essence.

Violet told herself that it didn't matter. Indeed, it was perfectly understandable, given the circumstances, but it stung and she found herself staring off into the distance, biding her time until everyone returned.

Which they did.

In dribs and drabs. The office filled out. The noise

levels rose. It was a young, enthusiastic and wildly exuberant team.

She didn't know whether Matt had said anything about her resignation, and she kept a low profile, but her eyes kept darting to the bank of lifts, looking out for her boss. When he finally showed up, well after she had had her lunchtime sandwich and bottled water, she had given up on him returning at all and was busy collating information that would be needed for a handover.

She was aware of him by the shadow over her desk, at which point she looked up, a professional smile pinned to her face.

'Apologies if you got here and found an empty office,' Matt said without preamble, before heading into his office. 'Did you get all those emails sorted and sent? Hope you used your time out productively. Can't have you shirking because you're on your way out.'

'All done.' Violet was her usual crisp and efficient self as she followed him into his office and shut the door behind her.

They usually spent at least an hour a day privately debriefing on updates on any of his many companies scattered across the globe. She flipped open her laptop, ready to start, when he held up one hand.

'No need.'

'I beg your pardon?'

'In fact, I'm going to have to get a number of the more sensitive accounts removed from your remit.'

Violet paled. She stared down at her laptop and felt the prickle of tears gathering behind her eyes.

'Of course.' She cleared her throat and quietly closed the laptop. 'If you make a list of them, I'll make sure they're transferred out of my portfolio.'

Matt relaxed back and lounged into his leather chair, hands draped loosely over its arms. He pushed the chair back and angled it so that he could stretch out his legs. 'In fact, maybe it would be better if you surrender your work computer completely.'

'But why?' She gazed at him in speechless consternation. She barely recognised the drop-dead gorgeous guy looking at her with bland, calm indifference. His hair was swept back, curling at the collar of his faded grey tee shirt. His navy eyes were cool and guarded. He was more of a stranger than the man she had met on the very first day she had walked into his office.

'Why do you think you weren't included in this morning's activities, Violet?'

'I had no idea there was a conference planned at all.'

'It was hurriedly arranged last night. A significant development with one of our smaller takeovers in the Far East sparked the need for a conference. I arranged it myself.'

'Because you no longer trust me,' Violet said dully. She stared at her fingers, long, slender fingers, fingers that had delicately begun playing the piano almost before she could walk. She could feel her heart thudding inside her chest and she wanted to choke.

'It's not about trust, exactly.'

'Oh, but it is, Matt.' Violet looked directly at him, her face calm and pale. 'If I surrender my work computer—and of course, I completely understand, and I'll hand it over to you as soon as I leave this office—how am I supposed to carry on here? Should I go to the stationery office and stock up on paper and pencils so that I can write everything down longhand?'

Just for a second, she saw a flash of *something* in those deep-blue eyes, but it didn't last.

'You can work on non-sensitive issues.'

'Like what?'

'Well,' Matt mused, tilting his head to one side and appearing to give her question a great deal of thought. 'There's always a lot of office rearranging to be done.' He waved a hand in the general direction of the industrial metal cabinet that stretched from floor to ceiling against the grey wall in his office, and which contained a ridiculous number of complex computer and coding manuals that were largely ignored by every single employee in the company. 'There's always that monstrosity. I bet half of those manuals are out of date. Could do with a complete clear-out.'

They stared at one another in silence for a few seconds, then Violet asked, in a low voice, 'Why are you doing this?'

'You work in a sensitive business, Violet. You must know that. I can't allow you to leave taking anything with you. For all I know, you might decide to set up shop over in Australia as a direct competitor.'

'You don't mean that!'

'You're defecting,' Matt told her bluntly. 'I have to take the necessary precautions.' He breathed out deeply. 'It's also naturally troubling that you've refused the job offer I made yesterday. Had you accepted, I would have known that your loyalty remained with me. As it stands…' He shrugged and let unspoken words settle between them.

After two-and-a-half years, he no longer trusted her. He was intensely passionate, intensely volatile and, yes, he would see her refusal of his job offer as a kick in the teeth. But did he really think that she was the sort to go behind his back and draw down on his contacts so that she could set up in competition with him?

That stung.

It was as if the time they had spent together had counted for nothing in the end. She shifted, smoothing one shaking hand over her grey skirt. For once, the uniform that had always kept those lines of distinction between them firmly in place seemed to be giving at the seams.

She felt miserable. She wanted to cry, but she wasn't going to yield to the temptation. For a second, she wondered how he would react. He went out with women who were clones of one another, and the duration of his relationships ran to more or less the same timetable. A handful of months, sometimes mere weeks.

And he didn't do any form of histrionics. Violet knew this because on a couple of occasions, a weeping ex had descended at the office and had been dispatched with ruthless efficiency.

They worked brilliantly together because Violet had always made sure to keep her emotions to herself.

Had worked brilliantly together, she amended mentally. No more. Now she was leaving and she had been dispatched with ruthless efficiency, a bit like one of his exes.

She didn't know how she was going to stick it out for the remainder of the week. It wasn't a long time, but it was long enough.

'Of course. When would you like me to start on the clearing out?'

'I'm having a late lunch soon. You can begin once I leave. Oh, and while we're at it, I've come to the conclusion that there's no need for you to work out any of your notice.'

'I thought… What about a replacement? I know a week isn't a long time, but I can already think of a few candidates for the job if we promote from within the company.'

Violet realised she was desperate to see a glimmer of the warmth he had always shown towards her and which she had always taken for granted. But his face was as cold as a slab of icy marble as he stared at her quizzically, before saying in a voice that threatened to turn into a yawn, 'Can you, now? Who are they?'

'I've made a list.'

'Of course you have.'

Violet smiled tentatively because this was a running joke between them, her love of lists. She said they were essential to make sure you kept up to speed on everything. He maintained that they were the sign of an uninspired mind and that life was too short for lists.

He didn't smile back. He just looked at her in a way that made her feel hot and bothered and out of her depth for the first time since she had started working for him.

'Maria Callway from Accounts.' Her voice echoed in the silence. 'She's very diligent and I know she would love the work. Then there's John. He's new but he's efficient. You remember he handled all those problems we had with the tech company in Maidstone a few months ago? Well, there's him. And Agatha Child would also fit the bill, and at fifty-two she's got just the right temperament for the job.'

'Right temperament?'

'I mean she's calm. Level-headed.' Violet filled in the blanks quickly. 'As is Maria.'

'Maria… Maria… Maria… Is she the one who's just returned from maternity leave after her third?'

'Yes. She has a brilliant eye for detail. If you like, I could call up their CVs for you to have a look at? I'm not sure whether we would have to advertise the job in the public forum but, honestly, either of those three would fit the bill and the move would be seamless.

They're all already familiar with most of the accounts, and you can...'

Matt held up his hand and Violet fizzled into silence and stared at him. Now that she was leaving, and within hours rather than days, she felt free to appreciate his beauty without lecturing herself on the idiocy of it. The only sport she knew for sure he played was table tennis, and only because there was a table in one of the rooms three floors down. It was always in use and many a complex problem had been sorted in between racket hitting ball.

Yet, to look at him, you would have said that he did nothing but work out. He was six foot two of tightly packed muscle and sinew, made all the more beautiful because of his exotic colouring. No one would have guessed that he was a billionaire several times over because the only expensive item she had ever known him to wear was his watch. She had gazed at that watch surreptitiously so many times, taking in the way the dark silky hairs brushed the dull leather strap.

Occasionally, and under duress, he was known to wear a suit, and his suits were all hand tailored, but usually his dress code for work comprised jeans—usually black—loafers—usually tan—and some kind of tee shirt, usually with a logo of sorts on the front. He liked rock, she caught herself thinking now as she looked from under lowered lashes at today's tee shirt which featured a prominent rock group from the seventies. No big surprise he had heard of her dad.

'No need to trouble yourself over a possible replace-ment,' he was saying now as he vaulted to his feet, tak-ing her by surprise.

'But…'

'I'll be back in an hour or so. Make sure you haven't decided to leave in my absence.'

'I wouldn't. Of course not.' She clumsily stood up but he was already heading for the door. 'I won't be able to get through much of that cabinet in the space of a few hours.'

He waved his hand dismissively, without bothering to glance back in her direction. 'Do what you can. Just make sure you're here when I get back. Oh, and you can take your work computer down to Hannah in HR.' He turned to look at her. 'Wouldn't want you getting any ideas about nabbing customer details in my absence.'

'Matt,' Violet said huskily. She rested her hand on his arm and just as quickly removed it. It was the first time she had ever knowingly touched him in any capacity and the feel of his flesh was as potent as the punch of a branding iron. 'Tell me you don't honestly think that I would ever do anything to undermine you? Yes, I'm leaving, but I would *never* be disloyal. I would *never* consider poaching any of your accounts. Never.'

'Duly noted.'

'I have no idea what that means.'

'It means that I didn't get where I have by trusting other people. After two-and-a-half years, you walk out with a polite one-paragraph email tendering your resignation, and it was only because I showed up at your house that I now have any idea about the person you are and the life you lead. When you discover you don't know someone at all, it's time to consider trust issues. So tidy up the cabinet, Violet, and don't worry about a replacement. I'll be handling that myself.'

Reeling from what he had just said, knowing that he was justified in saying it, Violet remained frozen by the door as he whistled his way out of the office and towards the bank of lifts.

When she faced the metal cabinet, she was grateful for the tedious monotony of the job he had given her to do, a pointless passing-the-time-of-day exercise because he no longer wanted her near anything that might be considered sensitive.

Because, in his opinion, she'd deceived him. She had a whole life that he didn't know about and her secrecy had caught him on the back foot. He saw her now in a different light and it wasn't a flattering one. Violet hated that, but what he saw as secrecy she accepted as just part and parcel of her personality.

She had been thrust into growing up when her mother had died and her father had gone to pieces. She had mourned in her own private way because she had had the job of making sure her father was all right and coping.

From a young age, there had been a gradual role reversal, and Violet had dealt with the responsibilities that had landed on her shoulders by gritting her teeth and getting on with it. She'd focused, amid chaos, on what needed doing—the practical stuff that had kept her father tethered through his wild drinking and drug-taking days. She'd focused on her studies, wherever in the world they happened to be as he toured, taking advantage of the internet and doing all sorts of exams online so that she kept up. There had been private tutors, but they had come and gone without much consistency. She had had to learn to depend on herself and she had.

And along the way, the simple business of opening up to other people, sharing and having a laugh about the things that happened to her, had gradually disappeared under the weight of her responsibilities. She adored her father, and she wouldn't have dreamt of putting herself first, but there had been consequences. Living surrounded by people coming and going, by the noise of guitars being played, pianos being tuned and drums being banged, Violet had learned the value of quiet. There had been few kids around her age who had hung around, so she had missed the phase of girlish confidences.

How was Matt to know all that, however? All he could see was someone who had been by his side 24/7 for over two years, who had decided to turn her back and walk away, and the only explanation had been forced out of her at gunpoint.

She miserably undertook the task allotted to her while mentally trying to convince herself that it was just great that she would be able to leave immediately.

Perhaps, next week, she might return to take some of the team out for a farewell drink, but then she thought of Matt coming along and she quailed.

It was after three when she heard the sound of Matt approaching. Noise usually heralded his entrance. People coming over to tell him about some new development, tech guys trying to persuade him into taking time out so that he could sample some new game or app that was on the brink of fruition. There was always someone who needed his signature somewhere and they tended to get increasingly frustrated when he chose to ignore them.

She looked up as the office door was pushed open. The job she had undertaken was far from complete and she was sitting amidst a pool of manuals, textbooks and pamphlets.

'You can drop all that,' he opened, strolling towards his desk. 'I have another job for you to do before you disappear to the vast blue yonder. Candy, meet Violet. Violet, meet your replacement.'

Violet turned and stared. Framed in the doorway was a five-foot-ten blonde who looked as though she had just stepped off the catwalk. Her hair reached her waist, a heavy fall of pale vanilla. Not much was left to the imagination with the dress code, and long, tanned legs were on show. Her eyes were a rich, bright blue and a crop top, barely skirting generous breasts, skimmed across her flat belly, proudly showing a pierced belly button. The piercing glittered in the rays of the summer sun shafting through semi-transparent blinds that covered the floor-to-ceiling glass windows.

'Ooh…' She did a full circle, admiring the office, while Violet carried on staring, literally lost for words. 'I *love* the office.' Her eyes were bright and enthusiastic and they settled on Violet with lively curiosity. 'You must be Miss Dunn.' She dimpled. 'Matt got hold of me from a friend of a friend of a friend and, as luck would have it, I was in between jobs. When shall we get down to things?'

'No time like the present,' Matt drawled, raising both eyebrows at Violet's startled expression. 'Why don't you show Candy the ropes for the rest of the day, Violet?'

'Of course.' Violet levered herself up, acutely self-conscious as she smoothed down the creased skirt and slipped her stockinged feet back into the neat black pumps. The blonde towered over her, five foot ten to five foot and an optimistic three and a half.

She turned her back on Matt. He had sauntered over to his desk and when she headed towards her office with Candy in tow, about to shut the dividing door between them, he called out for her to leave it open.

Violet glanced behind her. He was sprawled in his chair, feet on his desk, hands folded behind his head. His 'thinking mode', he had once told her. Right now, it was going to be his keeping-an-eye-on-the-potential-traitor mode, and she determined to don her best professional hat and ignore him completely.

The next two hours were painful. Candy, it transpired, was a friend of a friend of a girl Matt had dated four months previously, whom he had clearly met somewhere at some point and had stashed her name in that computer-bank memory of his for future reference. Probably as a potential date down the line but now, remembering her qualifications, as secretary material.

She was bright enough and enthusiastic enough, but she also asked sufficient questions about Matt for Violet to guess that it wasn't going to be quite the boss-secretary relationship he needed. But, hey, if he'd come to the conclusion that having someone decorative around was worth more than having someone less glamorous but a whole lot more grounded, dedicated and, frankly, *qualified*, then good luck to him.

Candy had very long nails, painted a brazen shade of pink, and Violet idly wondered how they were going to fare on the keyboard of a computer. She wondered whether the frantic clicking of long nails on the keys would irritate her notoriously short-tempered boss and promptly decided that it was none of her business.

'You can scuttle off now,' Matt interrupted them when Violet was just about at the end of her tether. 'And I'm talking to Candy. You, Violet, are to stay a while longer.'

They both waited while Candy rustled her possessions together, talking all the while, breathless, bubbly and very much like the women he dated...

'I'm not sure she's the right one for the job,' was the first thing Violet said as soon as they were alone together back in Matt's office, and the outside door was firmly shut against wagging ears and prying eyes.

'Are you saying that because I've put your nose out of joint by ignoring your words of wisdom and not taking on board the suggestions you so very kindly made?' He swerved round his desk, sat down and then pointed for her to pull up the other chair. 'Maybe I fancy having someone open and honest and… What's the word I'm looking for…?'

'Not really up to anything too complicated?'

'Eye-catching.'

Violet flushed and looked away. That hurt but, damn it, she wasn't going to show it. She breathed deeply, gathered herself and met those navy-blue eyes coolly. 'Maybe you do and you and Candy will have a long and rewarding relationship,' she said. 'But maybe you'll end up having to siphon off loads of accounts to Maria because, quite honestly, Candy isn't going to get to grips with that stuff.'

'Damn it, Violet!' Matt roared, leaping up so suddenly that she started with surprise. 'Maybe…' He skirted round his desk to stand right in front of her, all alpha male and simmering anger. 'Just maybe I gave in to the temptation to have someone bloody straightforward around for a change!'

'Keep your voice down!' But she was shaken because this was the first time he had ever raised his voice to her. He did it all the time. If someone fell short of his stratospherically high standards, he had no qualms in bellowing his disapproval. If he was frustrated, he was not averse to taking it out on inanimate objects.

But he had never directed his anger at her.

'Or else what? You forget that I own all of this!'

Violet looked down and didn't say anything, which seemed to infuriate him even more, because before she could start getting her thoughts together, before she could begin to make noises about clearing out her desk, he leant forward and gripped the arms of her chair, a suffocating presence that made her breath catch in her throat and sent all her thoughts flying through the window.

Her mind went completely blank. Her mouth went dry. Her pupils dilated and hot colour rose in a tide in her cheeks.

She could breathe him in and the woody scent of whatever aftershave he used filled her nostrils until she wanted to pass out.

'Do you mind?' she gasped and he glowered at her.

'Yes, I bloody *do* mind! Straightforward Candy is going to be a breath of fresh air after you, and if she takes a while getting there with some of the more complex issues, then I can always call one of your recommendations into play. Either the granny or the happily married mother of three. Or maybe the guy who has a boyfriend safely tucked away on the home front! Maybe I'm looking forward to having someone around who doesn't think that it's a gross invasion of her privacy to spend five minutes telling me how her weekend has been! Or that she might have a famous father who used to tour the world!'

Violet felt faint before the full force of his accusing blue stare. She wanted to shrug off his anger, which was understandable, given his temperament, but instead she just felt as though she'd somehow let him down in ways that were unforgiveable.

After today, she wouldn't be seeing this man again. He had dominated her life for over two years, had given her focus. He had trusted her completely and promoted her way beyond her pay grade. He had treated her with respect and admiration and suddenly she didn't want to quit his employ under a black cloud.

She didn't want to leave him thinking the worst of her, thinking that she had it in her to betray the trust he had placed in her by doing a bunk with his client base.

But she had turned down the best job offer he could have made, and to him that would have signified betrayal.

'You don't understand,' she protested, but without vigour.

'What don't I understand?'

'My life,' she said quietly. 'You don't understand my life. You have no idea what it was like to grow up with a rock-and-roll dad. You couldn't begin to comprehend how that made me the person I am today.' She was mortified at how personal the conversation had become, but she ploughed on anyway, knowing that it was her last day, her last hour probably, before she disappeared to the other side of the world.

Her head was lowered, but she could feel the force of his stare on her and it was hard to think. When she raised her eyes, they collided with his with shattering impact. His face was so close to hers that she could see the streaks of black against navy, the thick, lush fall of his lashes, the curve of his sensual mouth.

She was appalled by a sudden urge to reach out and stroke that lean, sinfully handsome face.

She balled her hands into fists and tried not to cower.

'I didn't accept your job offer because I want to make something of my music,' she continued in a barely audible whisper, nothing at all like her usual calm, composed, assured voice. 'I love playing the piano. I do it all the time. The piano was my constant in a life that was full of upheaval. Dad always felt guilty that it was a talent I never had the chance to develop, and he suggested that I try my hand at getting back into it when I'm over there. He knows people. I could give lessons. I'd enjoy that.' She took a deep breath and exhaled slowly. 'So there you have it, Matt.'

He drew back and stood up and, when he showed no signs of returning to his chair, she pushed hers back and stood as well, her dainty, slender frame a striking contrast to his overpowering, in-your-face masculinity.

'I'll go and clear my desk.' She cleared her throat and shot him a glance from under her lashes before edging away towards the door dividing their work spaces.

'You do that,' he muttered, flushing and looking away. He'd wanted to touch…and touching wasn't allowed.

Even he knew that. But, by God, that urge had been suffocating just for a second.

'And, Matt…' She waited until he was looking at her. 'I'll miss…' *You. I'll miss you.* 'I'll miss working here more than I can ever say.'

CHAPTER FOUR

WOULD HE VISIT HER…?

Melbourne beckoned because, as he should have expected, there was no such thing as smooth sailing. At the eleventh hour, one of his little baby start-ups, nurtured tenderly for months, had come down with a potentially life-threatening condition and Matt had to go and pay a visit because no one else would be able to handle the situation.

But would he visit her?

She had been gone for six weeks and he'd kept in touch because, after all, they'd worked together as a team long enough for him to recognise that they had formed a bond, and besides, what if she returned to London? It would be tempting to rehire her because only now that she had disappeared he could see just how invaluable an asset she had been. More so than he could ever have expected. It was as though she had taken up permanent residence in some corner of his mind and had hunkered down to stay. So, hey, he could drop in…

After all, Never Kill Your Options had always been his motto.

She had replied to his emails as politely and remotely as if she had been sitting across from him in his office, fending off those personal questions she had always disliked being asked.

Yes, things were fine. Yes, her father was doing as well as could be expected. No, she had not reconsidered his job offer even though, yes, it would have been convenient as it was a mere half hour away from where she lived. The weather was good. The food was good. The people were friendly. The scenery was pleasing.

It piqued him to think that she hadn't glanced back to the life she'd left behind and, were it not for his attempts to keep in touch, she would have galloped merrily into the distance in a cloud of dust.

He would look her up. Aside from anything else, it would be interesting to meet her father. Who didn't enjoy meeting childhood idols?

Just out of curiosity, he'd put a few questions out there, asked around.

He'd been a fan of her father. The guy was well known. Even though he'd binned the touring a while back, people still knew who he was, and Matt had almost struck jackpot on question one.

Scott Dixon, one of the owners of his newly acquired start-up company, had waxed lyrical about Mickey Dunn, who was a familiar name in the music industry.

He had recently set up his own small school for under-privileged, talented, budding musicians.

He was reportedly doing his first gig in six years at a hip, cool place in the heart of the city…with his daughter in attendance. As luck would have it, the gig coincided with when Matt would be there, sorting out his eleventh-hour road block. What were the chances?

He'd had a sudden image of Violet behind the scenes, always the carer, making sure her father didn't go wild. She would be dressed in her formal business attire and would probably be directing traffic with all the road-ies and fellow band members. He'd grinned fondly at the thought.

He'd debated whether to warn her of his arrival, and decided that he wouldn't, because who knew whether work would allow him time out to see her at all? Or even whether he *would* drop by. It could prove an awk-ward visit, best avoided. Rosy memories of his efficient secretary with the mystery background might be bet-ter left. After all, it wasn't as though theirs had been a social relationship.

Armed with a shed-load of preconceived notions of what he might find, Matt had not catered for what he would actually be faced with. He'd imagined a queue of polite golden oldies filtering into a venue that, despite what he'd been told, wouldn't be so much hip and cool as cultured and refined, befitting an ageing rocker who now ran a school for budding musicians.

Except, here he was now, and this wasn't what he'd

expected. Standing at a distance with the balmy night enfolding him, Matt surveyed the throng of people queuing and entering the exclusive venue. There was some rather stunning graffiti on the brick wall of the nightclub and two bouncers at the door, as though at any moment some disreputable troublemaker might attempt to barge the queue without a ticket.

He joined it. He knew from his research it was the second day of a two-day gig and he had only managed to get hold of a ticket by the skin of his teeth. Who knew that there would be so many old rockers lining up for a taste of the past? But then, it seemed that Mickey Dunn was quite the local celebrity.

He would surprise Violet after the concert. He imagined her anxiously sitting backstage, perhaps from a vantage point where she could keep a watchful eye on her father, making sure a bottle of beer wasn't slipped to him by some well-intentioned groupie.

Matt was the last in. The club was exquisite, lots of exposed brick, long, oversized mirrors and some more graffiti. There were tables on either side of the room, raised on podiums, where dining happened. In the middle, it was standing room only. On the stage was a piano, the usual drums and a couple of guys with beards warming up. Not original band members but, from the tuning going on, Matt could tell that they were going to be pretty good.

His thoughts rambled. He felt invigorated, which surprised him, because until the very last minute he hadn't been entirely convinced he would pay his ex-secretary a visit. Even more surprisingly, he recalled that weird feeling that had seized him when he'd been about to leave her house, when he'd stared down at her and it had been as though the world had suddenly narrowed right down to just the two of them, and something strong and urgent had been calling out to him to touch her. The urge to cover her mouth with his had been overwhelming.

He'd resisted, but with extreme difficulty.

Touching her, kissing her, thinking about making love to her... That was the stuff of madness, and he'd had the sense to steer clear.

But the power of temptation had left him shaken. Why had that memory leapt out at him from nowhere?

He almost missed what was going on because his thoughts had taken off at such a delightfully taboo tangent.

He almost missed Mickey Dunn coming onto the stage to rapturous applause. And Jesus...

He straightened. He couldn't believe his eyes. He stared and his mouth fell open. From the back of the room—and even though at six foot two he towered over most of the audience there, so that his view was uninterrupted—he had to blink to process the sight of his prim and proper secretary dressed like a rocker.

He thought he might actually have made a choking sound under his breath. Surprise didn't begin to cover his reaction. Gone were the prissy outfits he was accustomed to seeing her in. Not even jeans were in evidence. She was wearing a pair of micro denim shorts, black tights, biker boots and a cropped top, and her shoulder-length hair was braided into two stunted pigtails. She looked incredibly sexy, and he wasn't the only guy captivated by the image, judging by the wolf whistles that greeted her appearance on stage.

Her father sat on a high stool with his guitar, with two band members in the background. She took up her position at the piano and…magic happened.

The world fell away as he listened to old ballads, the words of which he knew, and cover versions of a handful of well-known numbers. He couldn't peel his eyes away from Violet, so absorbed in that piano, oblivious to everything around her. They ended on a couple of the band's best-loved fast numbers, old rock hits that had the crowd chanting and singing along. Violet was into it, standing as she hit the notes on the piano, and every so often smiling across at her dad who grinned back at her.

Lots of perspiration, lots of noise, the roar of approval from the crowd, then it was over and the lights were going down, and Matt legged it to where he thought the dressing rooms would be.

If he'd had any doubts in his mind about showing up here on the other side of the world, and making time to seek her out, then those doubts had been erased.

He'd never felt more alive.

He wondered what she would say. His mind was

filled with the image of her, so stupendously sexy. Some small voice was telling him that that was something he'd always known, deep down.

She was sexy underneath the prim suits, the glossy bob and the calm, unflappable exterior. Some part of him had always recognised an inherent tug on his senses, although it had only made itself felt when he had looked down at her in her house and his head had begun to swim.

They almost collided.

He was heading at speed through the carpeted corridors at the back of the club and she was bolting in his direction. She screeched to a halt and her eyes widened with a mixture of shock and disbelief.

'Matt!'

'Surprise, surprise.' He shot her a crooked smile. He'd forgotten how weirdly deep and melodic her voice was and how slight she was compared to him. An ache spread through him that silenced him for a few seconds, then normal service resumed.

'I've had to fly over here on business. Damned start-up has run into a few thorny problems. I don't have to tell you how temperamental three untethered men in a small boat can be when a big liner shows up to bring them to shore. All sorts of sudden doubts. While I was here, thought I'd drop by and see how you were doing.' He paused. Her cheeks were flushed, her eyes bright. He wanted to touch those pigtails, see whether they were real, because it was so out of keeping.

Violet flung herself into his arms.

The move was so unexpected that Matt temporarily froze. Just like that, he was acutely aware of every small curve, the delicacy of her slender body and her small breasts pushing against him. He gingerly put his arms around her in a stilted gesture that was part comforting caress and part bewildered *what's going on here?* hug.

Bad move, a little voice was saying at the back of Violet's head. *Very bad move.*

She could feel the way he had suddenly turned to wood, and she guessed that he was probably horrified at this crazy display of emotion from his otherwise buttoned-up ex-secretary, but she was just so relieved to see him that she could have burst into tears.

She broke free and began dragging him back to the dressing room.

'I'm so glad you're here, Matt.'

'Violet, stop. What's going on?'

'It's Dad.'

'What about him?'

'He's collapsed.'

She was half running and at those words he began striding more purposefully towards the rooms at the back of the club. People had gathered outside one of the cubicles and he forged a way through them.

'Anyone call an ambulance?' he shouted, looking around and clicking his tongue impatiently because they all looked confused and blank-faced, like a herd of terrified sheep in search of a shepherd.

'I did,' a timid voice piped up.

Matt nodded. Mickey had been propped up against a cushion. He was grey, wheezing and perspiring.

In that moment, Matt did what he did best—he took charge, and Violet watched.

She watched with blessed relief as he single-handedly cleared the room, having ascertained that no one with any medical know-how was available. He confiscated several phones from gawpers trying to capture the chaos on camera and, surprisingly, the phones were surrendered without protest. Such was the power of his personality.

She was shaking like a leaf as she knelt next to her father, stroking his hair away from his face. He wore a ponytail. She'd told him often enough that he was way too old for that style, but he'd steadfastly ignored her, and now seeing that ponytail in disarray was somehow heart-rending.

The ambulance arrived with paramedics and everything became a blur of activity.

'Want me in the ambulance with you?' Matt asked, cupping the nape of her neck and looking at her, and she nodded mutely. 'Good. But first…' He removed his jacket, laid it over her shoulders and shot her a crooked smile. 'Your outfit is great on stage, but you might be a bit self-conscious wearing it in a hospital setting.'

It was a gesture so touching that she couldn't speak for a few seconds, then off they hurried, out to the waiting ambulance that wailed its way towards the hospital.

'I feel so helpless,' she whispered once her father

had been whisked away and they were left standing in a room on their own like a couple of spare parts deprived of purpose.

She clutched at the jacket and dabbed her eyes with her knuckles. She hadn't even asked what he was doing here! He'd appeared as if by magic, and it just felt right that he was standing here now in all his magnificence, a rock in a sudden storm.

He was dressed as he always was, in dark jeans, a dark long-sleeved tee shirt and loafers. Casual and effortlessly elegant.

God, how had she managed to forget just how stupendously good-looking he was? How tall? How achingly sexy? She'd replied to his emails as briefly and as politely as she could, firmly believing that the faster she broke off contact with him, the faster her head would stop filling up with images that made her think she was losing her mind with missing him.

He was staring at her with concern and she chewed on her lip.

'Tell me what happened,' Matt urged.

'I wish I knew. He looked a bit peaky this morning, and I told him that if he didn't feel right we should call the gig off, but he insisted, and when my dad gets something in his mind he's an unstoppable force. But I knew he wasn't feeling well. I could tell every time he looked at me that he wasn't right.' Her eyes welled up. 'I know my dad so well. We should have called it

quits long before the end. I should have insisted. Now…
What if he dies?'

'He won't.'

'How do you know?'

'Because I have a hotline to the big guy up there.'
He smiled and Violet reluctantly smiled back and began
to relax a little.

It was amazing just how calm his presence made
her feel.

'I'm being feeble,' she ventured shakily. 'What a
coincidence that you're here. I hope the stuff with the
start-up gets sorted.'

'Forget that. Let's focus on what matters. Your father.
You go and sit down over there and I'll get you a cup of
coffee, even though a good shot of whisky would probably be more helpful. And then I'll hunt down a doctor
or a nurse or a consultant and find out what's going on.'

He was guiding her gently towards one of the chairs
lined up against the wall like soldiers in formation. She
obediently sat down. This, she knew, was a side to her
he would never have seen. The side that wasn't efficient, professional or calm under stress. The side that
was currently wearing next to nothing under the jacket
that thankfully he had given her.

She was vulnerable and tearful. She just wanted
to lean on him and let him take over because she felt
scared and fragile.

He appeared with a coffee, and then disappeared almost as quickly, and when he next returned he knelt in

front of her and tilted her chin so that their eyes met. Deep blue tangled with sherry brown.

'First of all, he's going to be fine.'

Violet closed her eyes briefly to control the emotion that single sentence had evoked. 'Did...did the doctor say that?'

Matt smiled. 'One doctor, a consultant and the chart which I insisted on inspecting. He's got, of all things, pneumonia. They're going to have to keep him in for at least a week and monitor all his vitals, but the general consensus is that he's going to be fine.'

'Stress.' The words were wrenched out of her. 'It's all been building up. I should have paid more attention, but my dad has always been good at hiding what he doesn't want anyone to see. He's been busy with a music school he started and then all the underlying worries about his health. He looked a bit peaky, and I know he seemed to be resting quite a bit, but...'

'No point in looking back over what you could or couldn't have done. Bottom line is that there's nothing you can do here right now. He's sedated at the moment. I'm going to take you back to your house.'

'No, it's not necessary. I'm perfectly capable of—'

'You're not and I am returning you safe and in one piece back to your house. You can don the secretarial hat another time. Right now, I'm in charge.'

Those words were like manna from heaven. She allowed herself to be gently led out of the hospital, as gently as if she were the patient and not her father. She was allowed to look in on him, make sure that he was okay, but that was about it, even though she would have set up camp next to his bed if she could.

She and Matt had arrived in an ambulance and now they headed back to her father's house in a taxi. The house sat on a magnificent plot of well-manicured lawn, a two-storeyed concrete-and-glass building with both indoor and outdoor swimming pools and a dedicated recording studio where her father spent a great deal of his time tinkering on his guitar, composing.

'Nice,' was the only comment Matt made. The drive had been silent but the silence had been companionable and now, as the taxi swerved into the drive and pulled up in front of the house, Violet suddenly felt a swell of panic.

'Don't worry,' Matt murmured, pushing open the car door but turning to look at her gravely for a few seconds. 'I'm not going to leave you until I know that you're all right—and don't tell me that you're all right. You're not.'

They entered a house that was a tasteful palette of creams and greys, interspersed with abstract art on the walls and colourful silk rugs on the marble floor. She could feel his presence alongside her and, whilst she didn't want him to go, not really, neither did she want him to stay.

She turned and their eyes collided, and her breath suddenly hitched in her throat.

'I feel so tired,' she murmured, fidgety all of a sudden. She couldn't peel her eyes from him. She was still wearing his jacket and she politely reached to hand it over to him. 'And you're wrong. I'm fine. Just exhausted. You don't need to stay here and babysit me.'

'Maybe I want to,' Matt murmured, his midnight-blue eyes guarded. 'I saw a different Violet Dunn before you left.' His voice roughened. 'I'm seeing an even more different one now.'

'I apologise,' Violet said stiffly. Her eyes skittered away from his face, but nothing could hide the rapid beating of her heart.

'For being human?'

The amused wryness of his voice would have been bad enough, but even more dangerously seductive was the touch of his hand against her cheek.

She curved her head, and it was such a simple, instinctive gesture, but it opened up the lid of that box she had kept so very firmly shut for over two years.

He lowered his head as she raised hers and the kiss was somehow inevitable.

The feel of his mouth over hers was electrifying. She'd been plugged into a live socket and every racing nerve in her body was suddenly and wonderfully sensitised in ways that were unimaginable.

She drew back, but reluctantly. Her body wanted more, but common sense recognised the need to slam shut the door that had been unexpectedly opened.

She couldn't meet his eyes and she stared down at the biker boots.

'What's going on?' she whispered. When she looked up at him, her brown eyes were filled with dismay and apprehension.

Matt raked his fingers through his hair. 'I'm asking myself the same thing,' he said gruffly.

'You should go.'

'Should I?'

Violet stared up at him. She wanted those lips on hers again so badly that it was a physical ache, spreading from her toes to her scalp and sending a wave of forbidden lust coursing through her.

It was the situation, all that pent-up tension desperate to find release, and Matt standing here was temptation beyond endurance. But, if ever a mistake were staring her in the face, then this was surely it.

She might not be his secretary over here, but she would be foolish to think that that made no difference.

Yet those lips… Firm and cool and so, so wonderfully sensual. And the way her body responded… It was as though she had discovered a network of nerves and tingling sensations she had never known she possessed.

'Matt…' Her voice was helpless and fizzled out into a strangled choke as he traced the outline of her mouth with one lazy finger. She caught his finger with her hand but the slight tremor was a giveaway that control wasn't completely within her grasp. 'This isn't what we're about.'

'You no longer work for me, Violet. You're shaken.

I get that. If you want me to leave, then say the word and I'm gone. Want that?'

'Of course I do,' she said weakly.

'I want to kiss you. You have the most tempting lips I've ever seen.'

'Funny, you've never said anything like that before,' she muttered, her skin burning.

'Would you have wanted me to?' Matt mused.

'Of course not!'

'You were like a cat on a hot tin roof the minute anything remotely personal left my lips.' He caught her hand in his and lowered his head to trail his tongue over her mouth. 'I would never have put you in the uncomfortable position of dealing with any advances from me. I was your boss and I have a lot of respect for what that entails. I'm not your boss here.'

No, she thought, he wasn't. And that opened all sorts of doors, all of which should remain very firmly shut.

The guy didn't do relationships and, when it came to guys, she needed the sort who did. She needed stability. In all areas of her life. She needed roots that could be put down and a guy who was willing to put those roots down with her. She wasn't frivolous or flighty and, whether he said that he was attracted to her or not, he didn't do serious. She should know. She'd seen his approach to relationships first-hand.

But her heart was beating very fast and her lips were tingling, along with everywhere else in her treacherous body.

'I'm all shaken up,' she muttered. She determined to listen to common sense because common sense was always right. 'Thank you for dropping me back and for... for coming with me in the ambulance.'

Matt shifted back and looked down at her with brooding intensity, his fabulous eyes veiled.

'I bet you didn't think that you would end up being flung around in the back of an ambulance when you decided to pay me a visit this evening.' This was more like it, she thought as self-control began to reassert itself and those unsettling, frightening feelings of helplessness started to recede. She couldn't quite meet his eyes but her voice was normal and habits of a lifetime were settling back into place.

So she'd kissed him!

What of it? Everyone was entitled to a moment of madness and she never, not once in her entire life, had had a moment of madness.

'Would you like a...a coffee?' She nodded in the direction of the kitchen and began walking towards it—half hoping that he would say a polite goodbye and head off, disturbing kiss firmly forgotten, half hoping that he would follow her into the kitchen, because this tingling, scary as it was, was also so wonderfully, tantalisingly exciting.

'That would be very nice.' Matt followed her into a high-tech kitchen where the only signs of occupation were the plates and cups draining on a metal draining board by the sink.

'Again. Thank you for being there for me this evening.' His eyes were on her. She could feel it. She tried not to focus on the fact that she was wearing an outfit best suited for a raunchy fancy-dress party. He wasn't her boss here and she certainly wasn't his secretary, and common sense only very thinly managed to plaster over that fact.

'There's no need to thank me, Violet,' Matt said drily. 'I'm very happy that I was there for you, although I'm sure you would have had your pick of volunteers for the role of shoulder to cry on.'

'What do you mean?' She glanced round at him, startled, and then handed him his mug of coffee, strong and black just as he liked it, and settled into the chair, facing him with relief.

'I mean you had a very appreciative audience. I'm guessing you heard the roars of approval when you walked in.'

'My father has a lot of fans still left.' She blushed furiously and sipped some of her own piping-hot coffee.

'I'll let that one go, but you know exactly what I mean. You looked the part. How are you doing over here? Your emails back to the home front are stunningly lacking in detail.'

Violet reddened further. Of course, he wouldn't know the effect he had always had on her, so would never guess that the paucity of her responses had all been tied in with her just trying to forget about him, which was the healthy way forward.

'I'm doing very well, Matt. Very busy.'

'With your father's school?'

'How did you know about that?'

'I have friends in high places.' His dark eyes were watchful as he sipped the coffee and he stole a look at her from under his lashes. 'I asked around, just out of curiosity. Your father has quite the reputation over here. Seems the bad boy of yesterday has become a pillar of the community.'

Violet smiled, relaxing, because this was the Matt she was so familiar with—a guy of such abundant, lazy charm that it had never been any source of wonder for her that he could attract women without having to lift a finger or make an effort.

'I'm not sure he would be comfortable with the *pillar of the community* moniker. He still likes to think that he's got a wild side left in him.'

'He's certainly still got the talent,' Matt observed. 'You played well together.'

'Were you surprised?'

'It's fair to say that pretty much everything about you surprises me,' he murmured.

She shifted and harked back to how he had reacted when he had seen where she lived, discovered a past he had never suspected—that fleeting look of betrayal on his face.

She wondered whether the fact that she had surprised him accounted for that kiss. She wasn't the woman he had categorised as his predictable secretary with no personal life to speak of. She'd broken out of the convenient mould and exposed a side to her that had taken him by surprise—and surprise, for a man like Matt Falconer, might prove a very enticing proposition. And then to-night, vulnerable and in her hour of need, she had revealed yet more about herself, as he had pointed out.

Could she, suddenly and unexpectedly, have provided an element of novelty that had roused the interest of a man drawn to the same type of woman?

Violet knew that she would be better off not giving house room to seditious thoughts. The more she tried to analyse the situation, and the raging fire that had ignited between them with such shocking speed, the more her thoughts kept returning to the feel of his mouth on hers and the responses it had generated.

Dangerous.

'You should go.' She dumped the cup on the table and abruptly rose to her feet. 'I probably won't see you again before you leave and I…er… I hope your trip over here proves successful.'

'Is this the bit where we shake hands and pretend we're strangers?' But there was amusement in his voice and, when he rose to his feet, he moved just a little too close to her for comfort. 'I've got a few days left here, Violet, and I wouldn't dream of leaving you to manage by yourself while your father remains in hospital. You can count on me. It's what any good ex-boss would do…'

CHAPTER FIVE

TRUE TO HIS word about not leaving her to manage for herself—a sweeping statement that had filled her with dread—Matt turned up at eight the following morning. Violet had already been up for an hour and was pointlessly pottering around the house, waiting for the hours to slip by before she could go to the hospital and visit her father.

'He's out of the woods,' she had been told when she had telephoned for information at six that morning. 'But he's heavily sedated and won't be able to respond to visitors for at least a couple of days. The body can take only so much stress and I suspect your father has been ignoring warning signs for a number of weeks now.'

She would go and sit by her heavily sedated father, she decided, even if he was sleeping and out of it.

She couldn't bear the thought of twiddling her thumbs. All the caring instincts that had been her faithful companions for so many years had risen to the surface. She almost felt guilty that her father had collapsed in such a dramatic fashion. Surely, she should have been able to see the signs of something more serious than him looking a little peaky? She should never have been swayed by his hearty reassurances that the concert should go ahead, even if he was a bit under the weather.

All this was in her head when she pulled open the door to find Matt standing outside, lounging against the door frame, his blue eyes keenly observant as she gaped at him.

'What are you doing here?' Instinctively, she touched her mouth with her fingers, an unconscious gesture as she remembered the power of that kiss they had shared. She dropped her hand and gathered herself but her skin was prickling all over and her face was red. She had been very grateful for his presence the day before, when everything had been in turmoil and her nerves had been shattered, but in the cold light of day, alarm bells were ringing in her head.

They had kissed.

They had broken a barrier that had been firmly in place for years. Now, out here, it was all a muddle and his presence on her doorstep was the last thing she felt she could deal with.

'I've brought you breakfast.' Like a magician, he whipped a bag out from behind him and dangled it in front of her. 'Thought you might not have eaten.'

'Matt…' she dithered, self-conscious in her cut-off jeans and small, faded tee shirt. She recalled the outfit of the evening before and shuddered. 'There was no need for you to come and check up on me. I'm very grateful that you were around yesterday, but Dad's settled, and I'll be fine.'

Matt looked at her with brooding interest.

Point taken, if he were being honest. There was no need for him to be here, standing on her doorstep with a bag of bread in his hand. He was no one's knight in shining armour, and he didn't do rescuing of damsels in distress, but yesterday...

Yesterday had been a revelation.

He'd gone to that concert as a token nod to the boss-secretary relationship they had successfully shared for over two years. Admittedly, he had been curious to see how she was faring. First and foremost, he was here on business, but she had departed British shores a slightly different person from the one he had boxed, labelled and filed away. And, yes, he had been curious to see how Violet Dunn Mark Two was doing on the other side of the world. That was the story he had spun to himself and he was sticking to it.

When she'd walked out onto that podium and sat at the piano, he'd stopped breathing. The crowded room had melted away and he had only had eyes for a woman who had shed the chrysalis and emerged a butterfly.

And then, to compound the impression, he had seen her without her customary veneer of efficiency and self-control. He'd seen her vulnerable and dependent and the combination had kick-started something inside him that had…brought him right here to her door. With a bag of bread.

'Are you going to ask me in?' He lightly rested his hand on the door. Violet sighed and stepped aside as he brushed past her into the house, heading directly to the kitchen like a man with a purpose.

'Tell me how your father is doing,' he threw over his shoulder as he dumped the bag of bread on the table and spun round to look at her.

Violet watched, noting the way he automatically took charge, the way he dominated and owned the space around him, the way he took her breath away—especially now, when she could no longer depend on the natural divide of him being her employer. They were standing here in this kitchen as equals and it was disconcerting.

To lessen the tension building inside her, she picked up the bread and began busying herself with plates and some mugs for coffee, directing him to a chair so that he could sit down and not tower above her in a way that made her nerves jangle.

'He's resting.' She wasn't looking at him but she was very conscious of the waves of intense masculinity he was exuding. She marvelled that she had been able successfully to withstand his physical impact for all the time she had worked for him, but then again a starched suit and patent pumps had been excellent deterrents for the devastating effects of her volatile boss.

Jeans and a tight tee shirt were proving a flimsy barrier, and the memory of that kiss was the icing on the cake.

She produced a plate with some of the crusty bread on it, dumped some preserves and a mug of coffee in front of him and stood back, her body language polite but unwelcoming. And he knew it. She could see that in his shrewd, amused eyes as he briefly looked at her before diving into the bread, lathering it with some of the wild lime marmalade she loved.

'Understandable,' Matt commented neutrally.

'I'm going to visit him…' she glanced at her watch '…very soon.'

'I'm guessing he's going to be out of it for a while.'

Violet narrowed her eyes and wondered whether he had somehow managed to prise information about her father's condition out of the hospital.

'I'm surprised,' she said, hurriedly changing the subject, 'that you're not at work. I know you've always liked an early start.'

'So much you know about me,' Matt drawled, voice lazy, amused, intimate. 'Your successor, capable though he is, lacks your intuitive feel for my movements.'

'It's something that comes with time,' she said briskly.

'But, of course, you make a valid point. I do enjoy an early start. My early starts, however, appear to have hit a brick wall with the guys here. Their preferred day starts at ten.'

'Tough.' Violet tried to hide a sudden smile because

he had always been impatient with anyone who didn't view rising with the larks as a golden opportunity to brainstorm or catch up on emails.

'Isn't it? Although,' he said pensively, 'it did mean that I could drop by here with this bread. Excellent bread, by the way, and I like the jam.' He turned the bottle in his hands and inspected the label before dumping it back on the table. 'Also means that I could take you to the hospital to see your father, and I've had some thoughts on the rest of the day.'

Violet's mouth dropped open and she looked at him in consternation.

'You're going to tell me that there's no need.' He waved his hand dismissively. 'But it's not an issue. I'm more than happy to be of help in this hour of need for you. You've spent many an overnighter with me, burning the midnight oil and ploughing through reams of legal paperwork that needed to meet a deadline. Never a complaint. So don't even think for one moment that this will be putting me out.'

Since Violet had not been thinking any such thing, she could only continue to gape at him in silence, temporarily lost for words.

As was his way, he had brought his own picnic to the party and was happy barrelling ahead with his game plan. Which was… What, exactly? What thoughts did he have for the rest of the day?

She quailed.

'Here's my plan,' Matt told her crisply, the consummate professional now, which should have been reassuring but somehow wasn't. He pushed his plate to one side and tilted his head to look at her appraisingly. 'We go to the hospital so that we can find out how your father is doing.'

'We? *We?*' Violet parroted faintly.

'You were in meltdown yesterday,' Matt pointed out. 'And there's nothing wrong with that, Violet. There's nothing wrong with having to lean on someone else now and again.'

Violet wondered whether she was now occupying a parallel universe. Since when had Matt Falconer ever prided himself on being a man that a woman in a meltdown could lean on? She opened her mouth tactfully to point that out, but he was gathering momentum, leaning forward so that he could direct the full blast of his concentration on her as he finished what he had to say.

'You probably won't want to admit it, but you will have woken up this morning just as anxious as you would have been when your head hit that pillow last night.'

'Don't be ridiculous.' She had, but she was sticking to the brief, because if she strayed too far from it—and kissing him the night before in a moment of weakness definitely qualified for that—then who knew what might happen? She felt faint when her brain started travelling down that road and she very firmly put the brake on it.

'I don't need you to hold my hand, Matt. I'm perfectly capable of dealing with this situation on my own.'

'Are you? Or are you just saying that because that's the persona you've always cultivated?'

'Don't try to psychoanalyse me,' Violet said sharply.

'Why?' He looked at her narrowly. 'So the boot, for once, is on the other foot. Why don't you relax and enjoy it?'

'I'm not your responsibility.' She bristled and shot him a fulminating glance from under her lashes. 'And,' she posed tartly, 'since when have you ever seen psychoanalysing any woman as something to put on your list of good deeds for the day?'

Matt grinned. 'I miss that. The way you can make me laugh. Most men would be cut down at the knees by that sharp tongue of yours, but it's always done wonders for my frame of mind. Moving on, though. We go to the hospital, where it would be pointless for you to sit around watching your dad while he rests. So my plan is to take you to the company, and you can dive in and help me wade through these last-minute stumbling blocks.'

'You want me to *work* with you?'

'Do you have other plans for the day?'

'Yes. No. I might.'

'Mixed messages going on here, so I'll interpret it myself and say that you have no plans except visiting your father and getting yourself knotted up, wondering if you could have done something to prevent it.'

He slapped his thighs and rose to his feet. 'Some

healthy distraction would work wonders for you and, as a bonus, you'd be doing me a favour. I hadn't planned on coming over here, at least not at this point in time, and there's more ego stroking, fine-tuning of detail and soothing than I'd banked on. The guys who run this show are like kids, and their paperwork, now that it's all been excavated for inspection, is in total chaos.' He looked at her seriously. 'It would help having you there, Violet. We've always worked well together. No reason why you can't take some time out to help me out now. And it would get your mind off things.'

'I will need to go to the hospital. My dad will need me as soon as he's out. I can't just drop these responsibilities to help you out.'

'At least a week,' Matt told her without preamble and she blinked and looked at him, confused. 'To clarify, I took the liberty of phoning his consultant. I thought I would come here the bearer of glad tidings. In times of stress, sometimes it takes a third party to look at things through independent eyes. You can count on me to be those independent eyes on your behalf.'

'You took the liberty of phoning the consultant?'

'Your father will be recuperating in hospital for at least a week, possibly a bit longer. He's in a private ward with the best possible care, but his overall health has been compromised over the years, so recovery will take slightly longer than might have been the case for someone younger and stronger.'

'You phoned and asked for an update on my dad?'

'No need to thank me. I thought you might be nervous doing it yourself. Bottom line, he's drugged up to the eyeballs at the moment and on a drip. He won't really be conscious of you being there at his side, at least not for the time being. He certainly won't be up for lengthy visiting and I doubt the hospital would encourage it. They want their patient to build his strength up, and he's sure to feel guilty about what happened if you're there 24/7 holding his hand and peering anxiously into his face.'

Speechless, Violet stared at him. 'You can't just appear on my doorstep and start micromanaging my life, Matt!'

'No, but I can provide healthy distraction.' He paused. 'Unless you have more pressing options, then I'm at a loss as to why you won't take me up on this offer. In a week, I'll be gone and you can carry on with your life here and your father should be back at home. You can devote all your attention to him then. In the meantime, where's the harm in burying your very justifiable worries into something productive and challenging?'

Where indeed? was what Violet thought ten days later. He had said that he would be in Melbourne for a week. His dulcet tones, and tantalising offer to take her mind off the horror of her father being rushed into hospital and all the attendant worry that went with that, had seduced her into doing as he'd asked.

Besides, she missed her job. She missed the adrenaline rush and the frantic pace of life. She missed being kept intellectually stretched. She loved her music, and enjoyed the freedom of being able to devote time to it—to help with the foundation her father had set up to give help, tuition and lessons to gifted kids—but she still missed the intellectual rush she had always felt working for Matt.

She'd agreed to work with him, safe in the knowledge that his time in the country would be limited. One week and he'd be off. That had been three days ago and counting.

Admittedly, there was a lot to do. They got stuck in. The very brainy, gifted but juvenile owners of the start-up had to be yanked down to earth at frequent intervals. Their lawyers were all university friends and conversation went off-piste at an alarming rate. Violet, attuned to Matt's personality, was adept at guessing when he was being pushed to the limits, and she liked being able to step in and defuse potentially awkward situations.

In between all the captivating, time-consuming and thorny issues that had to be untangled, Violet went to see her father. Sometimes Matt came with her and she was ashamed to find that she enjoyed those visits. Her father came alive in Matt's presence, opening up to his charm and his obvious enthusiasm for the rock history that defined him.

And they'd gone sightseeing. A little, here and there. Perfectly normal—except she was uneasily aware that they weren't a 'normal' couple, taking in the sights.

'I'm pretty happy to do my own thing,' he'd shrugged on the first night. 'I'm staying at one of the Hyatt hotels. There's a bar. Food will be available. I'm perfectly capable of lending a helping hand to people when it comes to getting them to talk to me.'

Violet could believe that. The man could charm anyone.

She was working with him, quite out of the blue, and that was one thing. It was quite another thing to start socialising with him, but the lines between them were now so blurred. And she was enjoying his company. She had forgotten how witty he could be. She'd not really made any friends out here and it was nice having an escort. One dinner became two, and two merged into three, and she began blanking out the issue of his departure, not wanting to think about it.

It felt good to talk about her dad. When she talked about him, surprisingly she found herself talking about her past, lulled into confidences that would never have happened when she had been working for Matt in London.

'I like the new Violet Dunn,' he had murmured the night before when he had seen her to her front door and had been about to take his polite leave, as he always did. 'Long may she live.' His eyes had rested on her, hooded and lingering, sending a shiver of racing excitement skittering through her.

She hadn't forgotten that kiss. It was never mentioned. But it had lodged there in her head like a burr, escalating feelings inside her that made her feel as though she were on a rollercoaster ride, soaring up and swooping down so that her stomach was constantly flipping over.

Now at six thirty in the evening, with business finally reaching a satisfactory conclusion and signatures all on paper, they were relaxing in one of the coolest bars in Melbourne. The curved walls were simply bottles of alcohol upon bottles of alcohol on glass shelves, and the lighting was mellow and subdued. They were sitting in two turquoise chairs, facing one another, and as yet the place was uncrowded.

'You've been invaluable.'

Violet blushed. She guiltily thought of all the other non-business entertainment they had enjoyed. At first, it had been hard to overcome her ingrained reticence, but it had been stupidly easy to move on from that place and to start enjoying his company. Way too easy.

'Thank you,' she replied huskily, then added tentatively, 'You were right. It's done me good. Taken my mind off…everything. And with Dad coming back home tomorrow and in such a good place, thanks to your bracing chats and positive encouragement, well, all told it was a good idea. And I've enjoyed getting back into the swing of working to a deadline.'

'The offer still stands,' Matt drawled. 'There's still work to be done now that the takeover has been completed. It wouldn't have to be a permanent situation. A few weeks, no more.'

Violet thought of having a link remain between them—exchanging emails, hearing his voice down the end of a line, even if the conversation was work-related.

'It's fine.' She smiled politely and bid a mental farewell to her momentary weakness. She remembered why she had known that walking away would be for the best. She remembered those stirrings of attraction she had felt, the way he had consumed her thoughts.

'In which case, this…' he raised his whisky glass in salute '…will be our last drink shared. I leave tomorrow. Been here slightly longer than anticipated, but needs must.'

She kept on smiling, but suddenly the bottom of the world had dropped from beneath her. She hated it. Hated the surge of fear that swept over her in a tidal wave. Fear of the void he was going to be leaving behind.

'Of course. I'm surprised no one's sent a jet over to ferry you back.'

Matt looked at her steadily, slightly twirling his glass between his fingers.

'I wouldn't have taken the ride back,' he murmured softly.

'Too much work to get through?'

'All Work and No Play has always been my motto. The play here has been too enjoyable for me to have accepted an early ferry back to base camp.'

'What do you mean?'

'You, Violet. I mean you.'

There was a potent, masculine charm he always reserved for women. She had never been in the firing line of that charm. She was now, and she licked her lips, nerves stretched to breaking point. There was no point asking him what he meant because she knew what he meant. She'd known it for a while, had sensed the frisson of electricity between them, had enjoyed it.

'This is my last night here and I'm going to put all my cards on the table. I want you. I want to go to bed with you.' He relaxed back in the chair, watching her over the rim of his glass as he sipped the amber liquid. They could have been casually talking about the weather.

'I…'

'One night,' he murmured. 'And then I'm gone. I don't want for ever. I don't even want tomorrow. But tonight… That I do want.'

Violet could hear her heart beating hard like a drum and the blood pounding in her ears.

One night. It was such a tantalising thought.

'Just tonight,' she whispered, barely able to meet his eyes.

'You know I don't do for ever.' He paused. 'I don't speak that language and I never will. No permanence, no cosy family life, no pitter-patter of tiny feet.' He had a rare moment of introspection, thinking of his own dysfunctional family life, of his parents, uniting two wealthy families, a complicated union involving assets and holdings. His father's grand country estate had needed his mother's lavish wealth. He had brought class to the table and she had brought hard cash. A perfect union on paper, but in practice, as he had grown from boy to man, what he had seen was the reality of a loveless marriage, and how a loveless marriage made for an unloved child.

'He'll never take over the estate,' his father had once said. Standing outside the formal living room, the fourteen-year-old Matt had paused and listened, every muscle in his body tensing at the dismissive tone of his father's voice. He had heard the clinking of glasses as they had drunk the sherry they always drank at exactly the same time very evening, brought to them by the butler.

'The boy doesn't want to have anything to do with the land. Might just as well not have had the little blighter for all the good he will do when it comes to perpetuating this legacy. Bloody disappointment.'

He'd wondered then whether his cold, silent parents would have stayed together had they never had him. Would they have gone their separate ways and searched for more than life had dished out for them? He hadn't stayed to hear his mother's response but something inside, already toughened over the years, had crystallised into ice.

If his parents were what marriage was all about, then he would always be better off without it. Sure, he knew that there were families out there who interacted and looked out for one another, but he'd never had that. Not only had he come to the conclusion that that sort of emotion was beyond his remit, but it was something he had no intention of seeking out. He'd stopped look-ing for parental approval, even though the search had pretty much ended long before then, and had devoted his life to doing what he loved and what he was good at. The land and the estate could go to any one of his useless cousins. He didn't give a damn.

Hell, where had *that* come from? Frowning, he slammed the door shut on memories he had little time for. He'd moved on from there.

'Sex, Violet,' he said roughly. 'One night. I want to make your body sing.'

She wasn't aware of nodding. This wasn't romance. What it was, was irresistible. Fantasy could become reality, a few hours of stolen bliss. How could she re-fuse? The prospect of playing with fire had never felt so good. She was barely aware of finishing her drink and making her way back with him to the house. She was a different person and everything around her was different. Somehow altered.

Everything changed when they were standing out-side her front door. Outside, night was a black velvet throw covering the world, capturing them in a bubble of heightened intimacy.

The trip back to the house had been a silent one, charged with anticipation. They had held hands in the taxi and Violet had felt sick with excitement. Now there was a thrilling urgency as he nudged open the front door with his foot and, before they could step inside the house and into a bedroom, he swept her into his arms and kissed her. A long, hungry, demanding crush of mouth on mouth.

She reached up and curved her hands around his neck. He was forbidden territory... She shouldn't be doing this, but then hard on the heels of that thought came another—she no longer worked for him—and, just like that, freed from the captivity of being his employee, and suffused with release from the tension that had gripped her ever since her father had been rushed to hospital, she freely gave herself to the thrill of the unknown.

He swept her up in his arms and began searching for a bedroom, heading up the stairs and pausing only to peer briefly into the rooms he walked past until he landed on hers.

He didn't bother switching on any lights, but the curtains were pulled back and the moon was sending slivers of silver into the bedroom.

'I can't believe we're doing this,' Violet thought out loud. She looked around at the familiarity of the room she had made her own since moving to Melbourne. She had brought over her most treasured score sheets and recordings of her favourite classical tracks, some by obscure but brilliant pianists. Aside from a handful of personal touches, the room was anodyne—pale-grey walls, a mirrored dressing table and cool, high-gloss fitted furniture.

'No? I thought it was pretty obvious over the past few days where I stood on the subject of wanting you...'

He had lowered her and now they stood, facing one another in the darkened room.

'It feels like we're breaking all the rules. I'm hardly your type. You shouldn't be wanting this.' She thought of the blondes who cluttered his life and she thought of herself, so serious, so adamant that there was no room in her life for a guy like Matt Falconer.

'Here's what I don't want,' Matt responded gruffly. 'I don't want you to think that I'm trying to take advantage of you because you're in a vulnerable place right now. That's what I don't want.'

'That didn't even cross my mind.'

'Good. And don't think that I don't fancy you. Trust me, I've never wanted someone more.' He guided her hand to his erection and Violet nearly passed out from the surge of terrifying, overwhelming craving that rolled through her like a tsunami, inexorably obliterating every single shred of doubt in its path.

He was so hard beneath the jeans and she was wet between her legs, hot, wet and aching for him.

And scared as well.

Scared because she had never done this before…and her inexperience was like a weight on her shoulders, stifling her desire.

She placed flat hands against his chest and breathed in deeply. She was shaking as she found herself propelled back towards the bed and, when her knees hit the side of the mattress, she sank down with relief and he sat next to her.

'God, Violet. Maybe you're right.' His voice was terse and he raked his fingers through his hair. 'Maybe this is madness. Tell me if this madness is something you can deal with.'

Don't look for involvement. That was what she heard in that statement. *Make sure you can deal with me walking away.*

'Don't go.' She circled his wrist with her fingers and thrilled at the latent strength there. She wanted to strip off her clothes. She wanted him to touch her so much that her whole body ached with it. 'It's just that…'

'You don't know which way to turn? Understandable.' Because she was what she was, he thought, and that was what made this so exciting.

'I'm a virgin,' she said in a rush before a lengthy guessing game could begin. 'I know you're going to be shocked. It's shocking. You want to know why. Well, it's because sex was never something that seemed to crop up. You once said that something got sacrificed when I became a carer. Well, for me that was normality. A life on the road and then being responsible for dad when I was young… Well, there you go. You should know.' She looked away, but slowly, by his finger under her chin, she was made to look at him.

'You're a virgin.'

Her smile and calm voice belied the tumult of emotions coursing through her. 'We do exist. In fact, I like to think we're pretty special.'

'Will you let me be the first?' And, when she smiled

and inclined her head to one side, he began removing his clothes, taking his time, completely unashamed, watching her as he undressed.

Violet propped herself up and stared. He was so beautiful. The fact that the forbidden was turning into reality was such a turn-on. She wanted to touch herself and balled her hands into fists. This felt right. There was a tenderness between them that made her want to give herself over to this man without inhibition, with complete trust and in defiance of the fact that she had never thought she would have her first experience of sex with any man who wasn't in it for the long term.

And this wasn't about her feeling fragile because of circumstances, either. This was something she had been craving for a very long time, something that had brushed like a feather through her mind every time they'd been together in his office late at night… Every time he had come close to her, had leant over from behind to see something on her computer… Every time his lazy glance had settled on her…

His nakedness, oh, so slowly revealed, staggered her. His beauty. His strength. The width of his shoulders, the breadth of his chest tapering to a narrow waist and lean hips. Her eyes followed the spiral of dark hair and her heart sped up at the sight of his erect, gently throbbing penis. He took it absently in one hand and played with himself while keeping his eyes focused on her.

He was so uninhibited.

She was eager and ready as he approached her. Fear

of the unknown still lingered, but excitement to explore it was greater, and her body went up in flames as he undressed her, stilling her fluttering hands, very gently easing her to a place where she didn't feel self-conscious at being observed.

He made her look at him and he talked as he removed her clothing with practised ease, his hands gentle.

When she covered her small breasts with her hands, he tugged them away and lay down next to her, idly toying with her body, smoothing his big hand along her stomach, her thigh, brushing his knuckles against her wet crotch until she wanted to spread her legs wide so that he could do more.

'I'm going to take my time,' he murmured.

'Matt…'

'Shh. Just relax and enjoy, Violet.' He flattened her hands on either side and levered himself into position so that he could pay attention to her small breasts. He licked her nipples. Her nipples were big in proportion to her breasts, and for some reason those perfectly shaped rosy discs turned him on like nothing imaginable.

He said he'd take his time and he did, licking and nipping, then suckling on them one at a time until she was moaning with pleasure. She pressed his head down farther and wriggled under him. Her mind went blank. Pure sensation replaced thoughts. His hands shifted to her rib cage and he journeyed with a leisurely lack of haste down her body, trailing his tongue along her stomach, circling her belly button…

One Minute" Survey

You get up to **FOUR books** <u>and</u> TWO Mystery Gifts...

ABSOLUTELY FREE!

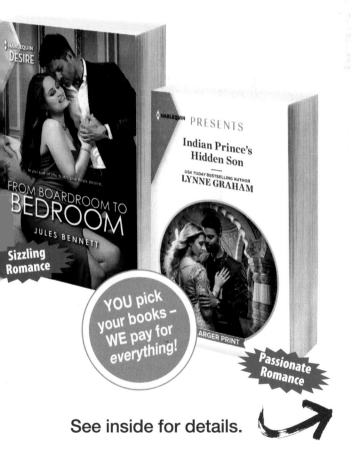

YOU pick your books – WE pay for everything!

Sizzling Romance

Passionate Romance

See inside for details.

YOU pick your books –
WE pay for everything.
You get up to FOUR new books and TWO Mystery Gif
absolutely FREE!
Total retail value: Over $20!

Dear Reader,

Your opinions are important to us. So if you'll participate in our f
and free "One Minute" Survey, **YOU** can pick up to four wonder
books that **WE** pay for!

As a leading publisher of women's fiction, we'd love to hear from
you. That's why we promise to reward you for completing our
survey.

IMPORTANT: Please complete the survey and return it. We'll se
your Free Books and Free Mystery Gifts right away. **And we pay**
for shipping and handling too! *We pay for EVERYTHING!*

Try **Harlequin® Desire** books featuring the worlds of the
American elite with juicy plot twists, delicious sensuality and
intriguing scandal.

Try **Harlequin Presents® Larger-Print** books featuring the
glamourous lives of royals and billionaires in a world of exotic
locations, where passion knows no bounds.

Or TRY BOTH!

Thank you again for participating in our "One Minute"
Survey. It really takes just a minute (or less) to complete the
survey… and your free books and gifts will be well worth it!

Sincerely,

Pam Powers

Pam Powers
for Reader Service

"One Minute" Survey

GET YOUR FREE BOOKS AND FREE GIFTS!

✓ Complete this Survey   ✓ Return this survey

▶ DETACH AND MAIL CARD TODAY! ▶

1 Do you try to find time to read every day?
☐ YES   ☐ NO

2 Do you prefer stories with happy endings?
☐ YES   ☐ NO

3 Do you enjoy having books delivered to your home?
☐ YES   ☐ NO

4 Do you find a Larger Print size easier on your eyes?
☐ YES   ☐ NO

YES! I have completed the above "One Minute" Survey. Please send me my Free Books and Free Mystery Gifts (worth over $20 retail). I understand that I am under no obligation to buy anything, as explained on the back of this card.

☐ I prefer Harlequin® Desire 225/326 HDL GNWS

☐ I prefer Harlequin Presents® Larger Print 176 /376 HDL GNWS

☐ I prefer BOTH 225/326 & 176/376 HDL GNW4

FIRST NAME

LAST NAME

ADDRESS

APT.#

CITY

STATE/ PROV.

ZIP/POSTAL CODE

© 2019 HARLEQUIN ENTERPRISES ULC
™ and ® are trademarks owned by Harlequin Enterprises ULC. Printed in the U.S.A.

Offer limited to one per household and not applicable to series that subscriber is currently receiving. **Your Privacy**—The Reader Service is committed to protecting your privacy. Our Privacy Policy is available online at www.ReaderService.com or upon request from the Reader Service. We make a portion of our mailing list available to reputable third parties that offer products we believe may interest you. If you prefer that we not exchange your name with third parties, or if you wish to clarify or modify your communication preferences, please visit us at www.ReaderService.com/consumerschoice or write to us at Reader Service Preference Service, P.O. Box 9062, Buffalo, NY 14240-9062. Include your complete name and address.   HD/HP-520-OM20

READER SERVICE—Here's how it works:

Accepting your 2 free books and 2 free gifts (gifts valued at approximately $10.00 retail) places you under no obligation to buy anything. You may keep the books and gifts and return the shipping statement marked "cancel." If you do not cancel, approximately one month later we'll send you more books from the series you have chosen, and bill you at our low, subscribers-only discount price. Harlequin Presents® Larger-Print books consist of 6 books each month and cost $5.80 each in the U.S. or $5.99 each in Canada, a savings of at least 11% off the cover price. Harlequin Desire® books consist of 6 books each month and cost just $4.55 each in the U.S. or $5.24 each in Canada, a savings of at least 13% off the cover price. It's quite a bargain! Shipping and handling is just 50¢ per book in the U.S. and $1.25 per book in Canada*. You may return any shipment at our expense and cancel at any time — or you may continue to receive monthly shipments at our low, subscribers-only discount price plus shipping and handling. *Terms and prices subject to change without notice. Prices do not include sales taxes which will be charged (if applicable) based on your state or country of residence. Canadian residents will be charged applicable taxes. Offer not valid in Quebec. Books received may not be as shown. All orders subject to approval. Credit or debit balances in a customer's account(s) may be offset by any other outstanding balance owed by or to the customer. Please allow 3 to 4 weeks for delivery. Offer available while quantities last.

▼ If offer card is missing write to: Reader Service, P.O. Box 1341, Buffalo, NY 14240-8531 or visit www.ReaderService.com ▼

BUSINESS REPLY MAIL
FIRST-CLASS MAIL   PERMIT NO. 717   BUFFALO, NY

POSTAGE WILL BE PAID BY ADDRESSEE

READER SERVICE
PO BOX 1341
BUFFALO NY 14240-8571

NO POSTAGE
NECESSARY
IF MAILED
IN THE
UNITED STATES

And then lower he went, and she inhaled sharply as he settled between her legs and began to lick along her wet crease. This was so unbearably intimate. She wanted to snap her legs together in prim rejection of his ministrations, but she couldn't, because the thrill of how her body was responding was too powerful. He gently nuzzled, his tongue easily finding her clitoris and stroking it until her soft moans turned into frantic groans and whimpers, and she writhed under him, plunging her hands into his hair and drawing her knees up, instinctively angling her body so that every sensation was heightened.

He didn't stop licking and, as he licked, he stroked the soft flesh of her inner thighs, driving her to a place from which there was no hope of return. She started to spasm against his questing mouth, coming with an urgency that seemed to carry on for ever until she could scarcely breathe from the power of it.

Spent, she drew him up alongside her, eyes wide and dismayed, because how could *he* be satisfied?

'You'd be surprised,' he said with a slow smile when she voiced her concern. He circled her nipple with his finger and, bit by bit, Violet felt her rag-doll body begin to stir right back into life.

This time, he guided her, and it was an erotic journey, touching him just so, holding his penis in just the right way, circling the throbbing head until he was groaning. He covered her hand with his. Her stroking was long and slow and then, when he could no longer take the mounting excitement, he pushed apart her legs and gently inserted his bigness, nudging his entry gradually.

She was so wet.

For a few seconds she knew that she was tensing but it was, oh, so pleasurable, feeling his shaft ease inside her.

A deep, urgent thrill bloomed inside her and spread out. When his thrusting became harder and faster, she was ready and tuned in. She dug her fingers into his back and arched up, eyes closed, feet wrapping round his lean waist, and her whole body splintered with wild pleasure as he came into her on one final thrust.

He sagged, lay completely still for a few seconds, then rolled off her to one side and shielded his eyes with one hand. When eventually he turned to face her, Violet was convinced that he would start on a litany of regret. She braced herself to assume a light-hearted response, the response of the controlled woman he had always assumed her to be.

She'd done the unthinkable, and was feeling the slow burn of delayed mortification, but when he spoke it was to say quietly, 'That is the first time I have ever made love to any woman without using protection.'

Violet didn't have to be a genius to detect the horror and alarm behind that statement.

'You don't have to worry, Matt. I've been using contraception ever since I got here to regulate my menstrual cycle.' Her face was beetroot-red because this seemed such a prosaic note on which to end what had been the most wonderful experience of her life. She turned to get off the bed, so that she could shower and give him permission to leave without a load of apologies and embarrassed excuses, but he drew her back down against him.

'Where are you going?' he asked in a lazy drawl. 'The night isn't over yet…is it?'

No, it wasn't. That was what Violet thought a month later. The night hadn't ended and it was never going to end. He had stayed another three weeks, then had left without looking back, and her heart had broken in two, but broken hearts mended and hers would mend. He wouldn't be around. He would never again be around.

How could she have known that there would be a price to pay for those stolen moments?

How could she ever have guessed that she would end up pregnant…?

CHAPTER SIX

'MISS DUNN IS HERE.'

He'd been expecting her. She had emailed him from Melbourne. A brief email which had made no mention of the time they had spent together. She'd politely asked how things were progressing with the start-up company they had worked on and then, as an afterthought, had informed him that she would be coming to London and wondered whether he would be available to meet. There was something she felt she had to discuss with him face-to-face.

For Matt, that could have covered any number of topics. Was she after the job he had offered her, after all? It made sense, because she'd enjoyed the adrenaline rush of working under pressure out there, but then wasn't that an easy enough topic to broach via email?

Maybe she was planning to return to London. Her father was back on track. Babysitting duties on the other side of the world could be winding up and it was possible that she might be after her old job. Trouble loomed on that front, if that were the case, because they'd slept together. Returning to their old relationship was not going to be possible. He hoped that she would have sufficient knowledge of how he operated to figure that out on her own.

Or maybe…

He relaxed back into his chair and thought, not for the first time since he had received her email, that she was interested in picking up where they had prematurely left off in Melbourne.

Regrettably, that too would be off the cards, because he knew that a casual relationship wasn't her thing, even though they had been lovers for a while and she had made no mention of taking it any further.

Sex with his prim and proper ex-secretary had been mind-blowing. He'd never known anything like it in his life before. The taste of forbidden fruit had been scintillating, had appealed to his jaded soul on a lot of fronts, but he was realistic enough to recognise the dangers of prolonging that brief liaison, even though he had been sorely tempted. He wasn't in the market for love and happy-ever-afters, but she was.

He would see where the conversation went, but there were few avenues he could think of that would be free of annoying complications.

'Shall I show her up?'

He nodded at his PA who, contravening all rules and regulations of a company that promoted an informal dress code, was attired in a natty pinstriped suit and a bow tie. His dress code was a daily source of amusement for Matt. He thought of Violet, and the neat and prissy suits she had been so fond of wearing to work, and he felt a sharp pang of nostalgia. He breathed in sharply and gathered himself.

'Give it five minutes, John. I have a brief phone call to get out of the way first.' He didn't, but for some reason, he felt unsettled and that wasn't going to do.

John nodded briskly and scuttled off, shutting the door behind him, and Matt relaxed back, fingers steepled, frowning because for once, his well-behaved mind was refusing to play ball. He realised that she'd been in his head, vaguely but persistently *there* ever since he had returned from Melbourne. It was an acknowledgement he found a little disturbing, because he had never been one to overthink the end of any of his relationships. What they had enjoyed, intense though it had been, was a moment in time, a brief meeting of ways which had always been very clearly defined as having an ending in sight. It certainly hadn't been a relationship, as such.

Even though they had got along extremely well. As they would, all things taken into consideration.

He found himself wondering what she might be wearing. In Melbourne, she had sported a far more casual wardrobe. Tight jeans, small tops, cute flat sandals…

The PA had been nowhere in evidence. He had a very pleasing memory of her playing the piano for him in next to nothing, and then forcing him to do a rendition of 'Chopsticks' so that she could have a laugh at his expense. He hadn't objected. They'd made passionate love afterwards.

He shifted, fighting down a sudden erection. He had no intention of picking up where they had left off, however much his body was tempted by the possibility, so why was he suddenly being bombarded with all sorts of inappropriate memories?

He opened up a file on his computer, a boring list of facts, figures and numbers, the sort of file guaranteed to numb a racing imagination, and waited for her to be ushered in.

Several storeys down, Violet was nervously reacquainting herself with the towering glass building that had been her home away from home for over two years.

She'd promised her father that she would be back as soon as she could, as soon as some urgent business had been dealt with, and he had been weirdly accepting. He'd said he was toying with the idea that a return to Blighty might be a good idea, now that he was as fit as a fiddle. No more drink, of course—he was over all that—but he could appoint someone to run the music school and keep the house on so that they could visit whenever they wanted. And wouldn't it be great to catch up with old friends back home…?

Violet had no idea what was going on. She had thought that Melbourne would give her clarity and cure her of her ridiculous infatuation.

Yet here she was and everything was an almighty mess.

When she had emailed Matt to tell him that she was coming to London and wanted to see him, she had opted

for meeting him at the office on the assumption that it
would provide her with just the right sort of businesslike state of mind she would need to deal with a difficult and personal conversation. Now that she was here,
memories were dragging her down. Everything was so
familiar. The memory of the simmering excitement she
used to feel every time she click-clacked her way to that
shiny mirrored lift was like a punch in the stomach.

She wondered what had happened to Candy but,
honestly, she didn't really care. She could barely think
straight and her nerves were all over the place as she
and John were whooshed up in the lift and, after some
halting progress through those familiar plush offices—
because so many people wanted to stop and chat and
fill her in on gossip—ended up outside Matt's sprawling quarters.

'I'll leave you here, Vi,' John said, and she thought,
in a panic, *Must you?*

She knocked and pushed open that all-too-familiar
door that led into the outer office where she had worked
like a busy little bee for such a long time. Matt's adjoin-
ing door was firmly shut and she took a deep breath as
she walked towards it.

'Come!'

Violet pushed open the door and did her utmost to
look calm and composed.

'Violet.' He smiled, but his eyes were guarded and
watchful. 'You're here. An unexpected pleasure.'

He'd been sprawled in his waiting-for-inspiration-to-strike pose, but now he sat up, smiling and indicating the chair in front of his desk. Ex-boss politely welcoming ex-secretary. He was uncomfortable, because he didn't know why she was here in his office, and she felt a pang of misery, because not so long ago he had been her lover, touching her in places she had never been touched and turning her into a woman she had barely recognised.

'I guess you're surprised to see me,' she opened, not quite meeting his eyes but not looking away, either. Just sort of looking through him and past him with a fixed smile that more or less mirrored his own.

'You have a house here. Should I be? Perfectly natural for you to return for a break. Brought your father with you? How is he, by the way?'

Violet, trying desperately to gather her thoughts, took her time sitting down. She'd put a great deal of thought into her clothes and was wearing a pair of black trousers, a casual baggy tee shirt tucked into the waistband and some sensible shoes.

'Dad's in Melbourne and, yes, he's fine. If it weren't for you, I might never have got to the bottom of his anxieties over his liver, so I must thank you for that. He must have spent months blowing everything out of proportion until he convinced himself that he was on the way out unless he had a liver transplant. A few words from the consultant taken the wrong way, and he could have been spared an awful lot of anxiety. But all's well that ends well. On that front.'

If they were any more polite with one another, she reflected, he would ask her to send him a memo as to the reasons why she had demanded an audience. As far as he was concerned, they'd had a bit of fun and that was the end of that. He was, after all, the guy who considered anything longer lasting than a nanosecond a commitment from which he was compelled to escape.

'Good to hear.' He paused. 'So, tell me why you're here—not that it isn't good to see you, Violet. Problems to sort out with your house?'

'I wanted to talk to you and I wanted the talk to be done face-to-face,' she told him flatly.

'Please don't tell me that you've returned for your old job.' Matt shifted, uncomfortable with the direction of the conversation but knowing that he had to be blunt. 'As you can see, the delectable Candy didn't work out, but John—one of your recommendations—is doing very nicely in the post. Would be very reluctant to put his nose out of joint by sending him back down to the bowels of Accounts…'

'I haven't come here to talk about getting my job back.' Violet surreptitiously wiped her hands on her trousers and licked her lips.

'No?' Matt tilted his head to one side and looked at her narrowly. 'What, then? I'm consumed with curiosity.'

'Matt… This is difficult for me to say…' She sighed. Her hair had grown just a little and she combed her fingers through it, eyes skittered away from him.

'Shall I help you out?' Matt asked heavily, suddenly restless, and she darted a look of astonishment at him.

'You know why I've come here?'

'If not for your job, then there's only one other reason I can think of.'

'I'm sorry.' She rushed into speech. He knew! And he seemed to be processing the situation with a surprising lack of drama, which came as such a relief, because it meant that they could have a sensible, unemotional discussion and then she could get on with her life. 'I wasn't lying when I told you that I was on the pill—even though you probably didn't believe me, because you made sure you used protection every single time after…after that first time. I *was* on the pill, but I was so sick after with Dad and everything… Well, I never thought that I would get pregnant, but I was wrong.'

He'd guessed. At least, that was what he had said, but if he'd meant it, then why on earth did he look as though the bottom had suddenly decided to drop out of his world? His jaw had sagged. His expression was the expression of a man who had just been sucker punched. His face had gone a deathly shade of grey.

'You didn't think that was what I was going to say, did you?' Violet managed into the ever-lengthening silence.

Matt managed to shake his head, but his vocal cords were still missing in action.

Violet wondered why she had been stupid enough to leap to all the wrong conclusions when he'd said that he knew why she'd turned up at his office from halfway across the world. 'You thought that I'd come all the way to London because I wanted to carry on what we had in Melbourne. Is that it? Was that why you looked so nervous when I walked in?'

She felt anger surge through her. She thought back to that expression on his face when she had walked in. Wary, cautious. She thought back to his demeanour. Ultrapolite and just the right side of amicable. 'You were braced to gently let me down, weren't you?' That dark flush said it all. 'Of all the egotistic…arrogant…!'

She shook her head and banked down the fury waiting to blow like a volcano. 'Don't you think I know better than to ever go there, Matt? We were two ships that passed in the night! Did you think that I would be stupid enough to imagine that there could ever be more to it than that?' She clenched her fists and tried not to succumb to the hurt of knowing that he'd walked away and had truly been alarmed at the suspicion that she might have wanted to tug him back, that she might have put him in the uncomfortable position of having to gently dislodge her like a stubborn thorn that refused to be pulled out.

'Pregnant?' Matt finally managed to croak.

'Yes, Matt. Pregnant.' His obvious horror had the effect of making her suddenly very calm. 'I'm afraid the pill isn't one hundred percent accurate. I had that stomach upset, if you remember, and as luck would have it I fell pregnant in that window when it stopped working. It wasn't your fault, but neither was it mine.'

'Are you sure?' His voice was cracked and barely audible.

'Yes.' One word. There was no point letting him think that there might be some mistake.

He looked as though the sky had fallen down, right on top of his sexy, unsuspecting head. He was clearly horrified, and she bit down the temptation to cry. Her hormones had been all over the place, but she wasn't going to break down here in his office because she felt sorry for herself. Because the dreams she'd had of having a baby had never involved the father of the baby looking at her as though she'd single-handedly made all his worst nightmares take shape.

He stood up and began to prowl the office, his movements jerky. Violet twisted in the chair and followed him. He was raking his fingers through his hair, staring down at the ground, then moving to peer unseeingly through the floor-to-ceiling window that offered such splendid views of the streets of London and all the stick-insect figures scurrying below.

He spun round and his eyes arrowed down to her stomach, which was almost as flat as it always had been.

Violet instinctively and defensively placed her hand on her stomach and cleared her throat.

'I have stuff to do over here, Matt.' She gathered her wayward emotions. 'I just came to break the news, and now it might be a good idea to leave so that you can process the information.'

'Leave? You want to drop a bombshell and then *leave*?' His voice was incredulous but she held his stare without flinching.

'I haven't come here looking for anything,' she told him, voice glacial, because she was still reeling from the humiliation of knowing just how badly he wanted to escape what was unfolding in front of his horrified eyes. 'In fact, I debated whether I should come at all. I know this is the last thing you would ask for but, in the end, I felt that it was only right that you should know.' Her voice tapered off into silence. If he had looked ashen-faced and shocked before, he was now beginning to look thunderously angry.

'Well, Violet,' he said in a restrained voice. 'How very magnanimous of you.'

'There's no need for sarcasm.'

'No? When you sit there telling me that you're pregnant with my baby and yet you're only here breaking the news because of a sense of duty, having manfully fought the temptation to just say nothing at all and... what? Bring the baby up on your own on the other side of the world? Spin a few lies when he or she got older and started asking questions? Maybe consign me to a premature grave so that the questions didn't start getting too uncomfortable? Is that how it would have played out, Violet?'

He was going to be a father.

Not for a second did he not believe her. He was going to be a father. And all of a sudden, the thought of any child of his looking back on his past the way he looked back on his horrified him. Yet she sat there, calmly informing him that she'd actually considered keeping this to herself.

'Don't be ridiculous. You didn't want me here when you thought I might have come to try to seduce you back into bed, so please don't sit there and start lecturing me about my decision-making process.' Her voice was strained, close to tears.

'No, Violet.' Matt purposefully walked towards her and then leant over her, caging her in, hands on either side of the chair. 'Ridiculous is the thought that you actually entertained the idea of keeping this from me, and whatever I might have thought when I saw you has nothing to do with anything.'

'Oh, really?' She tilted her chin at a defensive angle and stared right back at him. He was so good at making people cower, so good at using the sheer force of his personality and his physicality to intimidate. Didn't he know that she was clued up on all those tactics and had long since learned how to deal with them? Although, this wasn't exactly a work-related situation, was it?

'I'll stop lecturing,' he said tersely, 'when you start explaining how you could have thought that this was something you could keep from me!'

'You're towering over me and it's making me nervous.'

'God, woman! You could try the patience of a saint!'

'Which is one thing you're not,' Violet returned swiftly.

He made an inarticulate sound under his breath and drew back, then he dragged his chair around his desk and positioned it right next to hers. He was no longer towering over her, but neither was he a safe distance away.

'Have you *ever* thought about having a family, Matt?'

He frowned and glowered. 'What does that have to do with anything?'

'You asked me how I could have the temerity to even consider, for five seconds, not telling you that I was pregnant. Here's how. You don't do commitment. You don't really do relationships, at least not significant relationships. And you certainly don't do having kids and playing happy families. What you do are three-month flings that all end in bouquets of flowers from a flower shop in Knightsbridge.'

And, she wanted to tack on, *let's not forget that you are the guy who made it patently clear that there would be no follow-up to our fling because what you were after was a passing liaison. Don't you go forgetting that!*

He flushed darkly and sat back, his long legs sprawled apart. He folded his arms and glared.

Violet summoned all her willpower and returned his glower with cool, calm eyes. The power of his looks was always enough to make her heart skip a beat, and it was no different now, but she had to focus.

She had to erase memories of that blissful bubble

they had occupied in Melbourne when they had been lovers, holding hands and doing all the stuff that loved-up couples do. For a while back then, she had managed to forget that they weren't a normal loved-up couple. For a while, she had managed to forget that Matt Falconer hadn't been with her because he loved her, but because he had been intrigued at the new and very different side to her he had seen for the first time in his life. He had been with her because of her novelty value and that novelty value had kicked in the minute he had sussed that she was actually a three-dimensional woman and not the cardboard cut-out who had spent two-and-a-half years at his beck and call.

'Well, this isn't going to be one of those, is it?' he muttered darkly.

'Like I said, I didn't come here for anything, and I'm not expecting anything. I came because I felt you had to know that you were going to be a father. I'm not about to pressure you into doing anything.'

'This isn't the place to discuss the situation. I can't have this conversation in my office. It's not a business transaction.'

Violet wanted to tell him that it pretty much was, considering emotions weren't involved, at least not on his part.

On her part...

All sorts of emotions were involved. On her part, emotions had been involved for some time when it came to her charismatic boss and three weeks spent in his company, three weeks of making love and pretending that reality was something that could be put on hold for ever, had deepened the swirl of feelings inside her that she had always had for him.

She was in a dangerous place and she was brave enough to acknowledge that that was part of the reason why she had actually considered keeping the pregnancy to herself.

She thought back now, not for the first time, to that very moment when it had dawned on her that her period hadn't come. She'd been merrily continuing with her contraception but, when something should have happened, nothing had. Even so, she had bought that pregnancy-testing kit without thinking that it would actually deliver that positive line.

Of course, it was something that had had to be ruled out, but as she'd waited those few minutes for a result she hadn't really been nervous at all.

And then everything had changed. In a heartbeat, her whole life had been turned on its head. Her blood had run hot, then cold, and in her fancy en-suite bathroom she had suddenly felt as though someone had taken a bat and swiped her behind her knees. She'd wanted to collapse. The unexpected had happened and nothing in her life had prepared her for it, even though she had lived a life full of the unexpected.

But she'd had time to take stock. He hadn't. No wonder he could barely compute what she'd dropped in his lap.

She'd never witnessed him grappling with anything. He was always so dynamic, so in control, whatever happened to be dished up.

Before she could say anything, he was heading for his door and pulling it open, leaving her no option but to follow him.

'Where are we going?'

'My place.'

'I don't want to go there.'

'Tough, Violet. I didn't wake up this morning wanting to discover that I'm going to be a daddy.'

Tears threatened. Of course, he was only speaking his mind, but still it hurt.

She'd never been to his house. Never. The thought of seeing him in his personal space was disturbing even though she had quickly grown accustomed to him seeing her in her personal space in Melbourne.

He summoned his driver, who appeared outside to meet them in a black, low-slung BMW, and she allowed him the silence of his thoughts as the car manoeuvred through the crowded roads, heading out of the city towards the calmer suburbs of west London.

She'd expected a house. Something substantial. But he lived in an apartment. It was a massive apartment and very minimalist. Lots of white and a feeling of something begun but not quite completed. There was minimalist and then there were walls in search of paintings.

It was completely open plan, and as he headed for

the kitchen, where he briefly seemed to contemplate the restorative qualities of alcohol before settling on coffee, she took time to look around her. He offered her coffee but she went for water.

As befitting an IT guru, there were lots of gadgets. She spotted a couple of computers, an elaborate games console and a mound of games. The television on the wall was ridiculously large. There were papers randomly strewn on a glass table and on the silk rug by the white leather sofa, as though he had lain down to read through some work, got bored and decided to shove everything on the ground next to him. The place was so essentially *him* that she felt her heart constrict.

'Of course, it's pointless telling me that you didn't show up to ask for anything. You realise that, don't you?' This as he moved towards the leather sofa and sat down, pushing a couple of files to one side and then tugging what looked like a priceless, one-off glass-and-beaten-metal table towards him with his foot. 'And please, Violet, sit down. We have to talk, so there's no point standing there like a sergeant major about to break ranks.'

Violet shuffled over to a chair and uncomfortably sat down facing him. 'You didn't ask for this situation.' She could feel a wave of nausea roll over her. Morning sickness, but hers lasted most of the day, and dealing with it was a daily challenge.

'You're right. I didn't. But here we are. *Fait accompli*, so to speak, so what do you think we should do about it? I know. You tell me what you think should happen next in this scenario and we'll see whether your prediction coincides with mine.'

'This isn't a game, Matt.'

'Trust me. I'm being deadly serious. So? You came here, fuelled with a sense of obligation, and you must have had thoughts as to what would happen once you'd dropped the grenade.'

Violet bit down on an explosive response to that statement because every single word of it got on her nerves. But exploding wasn't going to solve anything, so she inhaled deeply and kept her voice well modulated.

'I suppose I thought you might be relieved to be released from having to engage…if that's the right word. Naturally, if you wanted, say, to contribute financially, then that would be up to you, but it wouldn't be necessary at all as I'm quite solvent. I don't think a baby would exactly fit snugly into your lifestyle, but of course, you would be more than welcome to arrange… er…to visit whenever you wanted. I thought the discussion might go a bit like that.'

Why was he looking at her as though she'd just insulted him?

'Interesting… You basically tell me that I can walk away, throw me a couple of options—just in case, on the off-chance I don't go for the abandonment option—and I thank you and see you to the door so that I can have a few weeks to think things over…?'

'No, of course not.'

'Because that's how it's sounding to me. I'm a commitment-phobe who wouldn't want anything to do with a baby I hadn't planned on having. Ergo, I would abnegate all responsibility. God, Violet, I thought you might know me a little better than that.'

He sat forward so suddenly that she started back and stared at him. There was simmering outrage on his face. Gone was the lazy, teasing guy and gone was the urbane, clever raconteur. Gone was the sexy man who could enthral her with his conversation and his wit. This man with the harsh, flat eyes was deadly serious, and she returned his flinty stare uneasily.

'I won't be stuffing some money into an account now and again to ease a guilty conscience. Nor will I be haggling over when I get to see my child. No, Violet, that's not how it's going to work at all. Here's the thing— I may not have bargained on being a father but, now that it's staring me in the face, then I intend to accept responsibility fully and without compromise. Full-time fatherhood. One hundred percent involvement. I won't be conveniently disappearing, leaving you to carry on and do your own thing. I happen to place a great deal of worth on the importance of being an engaged parent!'

Violet knew that her mouth was hanging open. She'd never heard him talk like this before, not in this tone, not with this urgency or searing honesty. His eyes were blazing and angry. Although, she really had no idea what, exactly, he was trying to say. Did he want to sort out visiting rights here and now? Maybe get her to sign something? Or worse…

'I'm not going to hand my baby over to you, Matt…' She blanched, sick at the thought that this might end up as a fight through the courts with an innocent baby as the end prize.

'Did you hear me ask you to?'

'Then I don't understand what you're trying to say.'

'Marriage, Violet. A ring on your finger and a walk up the aisle. That's where I'm going with this.'

'Don't be ridiculous.' Her head was swimming. He'd asked her how she'd thought this conversation would go. The answer was…*not like this.* In what world had she ever seen him as the sort of guy who might want a hands-on relationship with a child he hadn't asked for? There was commitment, and then there was *commitment*, and this definitely belonged to category number two. The sort of bone-deep commitment you took on board for life—no goodbye flowers, no divorce, no *it's been nice knowing you.* How the hell was she supposed to have assumed that he would want to dive head first into waters he had never been called upon to sample?

'And sooner rather than later. In fact, as soon as possible would work for me. Where does your father stand on this? Have you told him that you're pregnant?'

'Yes, just before I left, but…'

'He'll have to move over here. At least, if he wants to be with you.'

'Matt, you're not listening to what I'm trying to say!'

'Oh, I know exactly what you're trying to say, Violet. I'm just choosing to ignore it because we're both in the same position. Neither of us asked for this, but it's happened, and both of us are going to step up to the plate and accept responsibility—because to let a child pay the price of starting life in a tug of war between two parents would be unconscionable.'

'I have no intention of marrying someone for the sake of a baby! That's not how it's done these days, Matt!' Of course, in an ideal world, two parents were always going to be better than one—but two *loving* parents, voluntarily sharing the responsibility for the child they had created. She'd benefitted from having two parents, if only for a brief moment in time. Her dad had adored her mother. She assumed, although she didn't know for sure, that Matt likewise was the product of a happily married couple as volatile, charismatic and energised as he was. Which was why he would place so much store on them staying together for the sake of the baby she was carrying.

But, she thought, what about her? And was that the sort of forced relationship that would benefit a child, anyway?

'In all the times I thought about marriage,' she said, 'it was never with a reluctant partner who was dragged into it, kicking and screaming, because I'd accidentally ended up pregnant. And you, Matt—you must surely feel the same as I do? You must have wanted something more than to find yourself having to propose marriage to a woman you would never normally be with…' She lowered her eyes and balled her small hands into fists.

'Don't underestimate the power of your sex appeal,' he muttered roughly. 'And, just for the record, I never pictured myself being married at all, so, no. No romantic fantasies swirling in my head that are now being put to rest because of this situation.'

He vaulted upright and restlessly paced the room, as though in the grip of a power surge he couldn't resist. He paused eventually but remained standing over her. 'It must have been a shock for you,' he said gruffly. He thought of her realising that she was pregnant, alone and doubtless afraid, and he was swamped by a feeling of confusing tenderness that had nothing to do with the baby.

Violet looked up at him. This was what he did so well. Alongside that forceful, driving personality was an ability to empathise that reminded you just how complex and three-dimensional a man he was.

'Of course,' she muttered. 'I never expected anything like this. I'm not like you. I *did* picture myself being married one day, having kids. I just never…'

'Imagined that it would be with someone like me, Violet?'

Violet looked away. Her heart was beating inside her like a drum. Someone like him? If only he knew! She might have idly dreamt of being with Mr Ordinary, who would have been such an antidote to the nomadic life she had endured growing up, but reality had decided to take her down a somewhat different route.

He wanted to marry her, and for a moment she took time out to think about what a life with that might look like. Lazy Sunday mornings lying in bed, laughing at those silly jokes of his... Cooking together... Making love whenever and wherever... And then, when the baby came, parenthood with all its ups and downs, but parenthood as a couple...

It was seductive, but Violet knew that it was the stuff of fantasy. The reality was that she would be hitching her wagon to a guy who had never planned marriage and basically found it impossible to sustain a relationship with any woman for longer than five seconds. He couldn't do that with women he was genuinely attracted to, so what were *her* chances? How long would it take for him to get bored of her, baby or no baby? And then what? Would he fool around behind her back? Or would he become a long-suffering partner, eventually resentful and bitter for having been forced into a marriage he hadn't banked on? Both prospects appalled her because to become dependent on someone only for them to let you down... There could be nothing worse. Her father had let her down. Yes, she had coped, because she adored him, but he had let her down. She wasn't going to be let down again.

'Yes.' She took the plunge, killing rosy dreams of what would never be. 'You can say what you like, Matt, but it wouldn't be fair on a child for us to be harnessed

together, always thinking that we could have been happier with other partners if I hadn't fallen pregnant.'

'Oh, but, Violet…' His voice thickened and she shiv-
ered as their eyes tangled. 'You make a union between
us sound like such a catastrophe in the making, but we
both know that it wouldn't be all bad…'

CHAPTER SEVEN

HE CAME CLOSE. He touched her. Just a light, fleeting touch, the brush of his finger on her cheek, but it was enough to make her breath hitch in her throat. Her eyelids fluttered and she inhaled on a sigh, quite unable to control her response.

'See what I mean?' he murmured persuasively. 'One minute you're giving rousing speeches about our unsuitability, and the next minute you're quivering for me.'

'I am *not* quivering for you!' She was alarmed at the undercurrent of weakness she could detect in that protest.

'I still want you, Violet.'

'No.' She shook her head. 'That's not the point.'

'We get married and no one is going to say that the sex isn't going to sizzle.'

'Sizzling sex vanishes after a while. You know that.' She clicked her tongue but her skin was burning from where he had touched her, and her head was awash with hot memories of their brief, intense time together in Melbourne. 'Look at what happens when the sizzling sex fizzles out like a burnt-out firecracker, Matt. It's *bye-bye, it's been good knowing you* time. That's fine when it's just another five-minute relationship, but when two people are tied together by marriage, when there's a child involved, well, the burnt-out firecracker begins to look like a pretty bad idea.'

'None of my girlfriends happened to be pregnant,' he fired back.

'And because I am doesn't mean that marriage is the only solution, however much hands-on time you would want to have with our child. It doesn't mean that you're not going to get bored when the firecracker burns out.'

Matt's jaw tightened with frustration. On the surface, what she said made sense. It was true. Sizzling sex always had a tendency to turn to ashes in the blink of an eye, but this wasn't the same, and he was staggered that she couldn't see that. That a child being involved made all the difference. A child would make staying power the essence, the sizzling sex a bonus.

She wasn't just another woman to him—which was, somehow, what she was trying to say. She was the mother of his child… He frowned as thoughts tried to rearrange themselves in his head. More than that, she was…hell!…more than just someone who had shared his bed. Much more.

His thoughts screeched to a stop before they could gather pace and travel down that unexplored road.

'Marriage is about more than what makes logical sense on a piece of paper. Successful marriages are based on love and a loving background is what a child deserves.' She looked down. She had a fleeting vision of what it might be like if he really loved her. Perfect.

She raised serious brown eyes to him. 'I don't know anything about your background,' she said. 'I've worked with you for over two years, and I know everything about your take on relationships, but I don't know anything about your childhood. It's ironic that I was always the reserved one and yet you now know everything there is to know about me. I saw my dad fetching photos out to show you when he thought my back was turned. Back from hospital, and in the space of a handful of days before you left, he manages to bore you with stories about me and show you pictures of me growing up.'

'Who said I was bored? He's a proud dad. He may have been a wild dad who was fond of going off the rails but, one look at the way the two of you interact, and it's easy to see that you both adore one another. I liked seeing pictures of you as a kid. You looked serious even then. Hair in pigtails, frowning at the camera. All that was missing was a pair of specs. Think that paternal pride counts for nothing?'

'I never said that!'

'Think it's okay to deprive me of that experience because marriage is more than what makes sense on a piece of paper? Do you imagine that I wouldn't want to have the chance to love my child? To be there for him or her?'

'You're twisting my words!'

'You tell me that part-time parenting is acceptable. Would you be applauding that slice of wisdom if you were the one doing the part-time parenting?'

'You told me that there was no way you would try and…and…'

'In an ideal world, there would be no lines drawn in the sand between us, given the situation,' Matt told her coldly. 'But the scenario you have in mind has nothing to do with an ideal world.'

'I'm being realistic.'

'You're being selfish.'

'You're not even a family man!' Violet protested heatedly.

No, Matt thought, he wasn't. Never had been. When you grew up without the warmth of a family unit, when the people you turned to were strangers in an expensive boarding school paid to take the hit, then dreams of cosy sing-songs round the piano with loved ones never even registered on the radar once you reached a certain age.

But here he was, facing the family unit he had never courted. More than anything else, he wanted to make sure that his own flesh and blood didn't *lack* the way he had. He wanted to be the buffer for his child against the slings and arrows of life, which was something he didn't feel he'd had. He wanted to make sure that the past never repeated itself. The remoteness of his wealthy parents had felt like a wall of ice around him, and there was no way he wasn't going to do his damnedest to make sure *he* was there for this child. Being sidelined wasn't going to work. Neither, he thought with mounting frustration, was trying to strong-arm the stubborn, sexy, mulish woman glaring at him.

'Don't push me on this, Violet,' he rasped, but his eyes drifted down her body and he felt an ache in his groin as memories of their passionate lovemaking surfaced.

Violet sensed some infinitesimal shift in atmosphere and her eyes widened. 'Matt, I think it's time I headed back home. I know you mean well, offering to defuse this hand grenade by putting a ring on my finger, but I have no intention of letting you pay such a high price for a situation you didn't see coming.'

'Jesus, Violet!'

Time to go, Violet decided. She stood up, but suddenly the world was doing a giddy twirl and the ground no longer felt quite so steady under her feet. She swayed and in one leap Matt was there by her side. When he spoke, his voice was laced with urgency.

'What's wrong?' This as he lifted her off her feet and began carrying her out of the sitting room and towards a bank of rooms sprouting from either side of the wide, wooden-floored corridor. 'I'm calling a doctor.'

'No!' She didn't bother trying to struggle free. The light-headed feeling was abating, but one look at his face and she could see that he was worried sick.

In an instant, she realised that his marriage proposal wasn't just the gesture of someone resentfully doing something through a sense of obligation because that was how he had been brought up. No. This was his baby, and he genuinely wanted to be there to see things through from beginning to end, and that gave her pause for thought. His concern might not be for *her*, but should she deprive him of the opportunity to be a full-time father because she wanted more from him than he could ever give?

Was she, as he had said, being selfish?

She could see all sorts of complications from a relationship that wasn't grounded in love, but was his black-and-white approach really one she should take? Sometimes a person could become paralysed when they overthought a situation.

Her breathing was shallow as he gently levered her onto the bed. His bed. Giddiness and nausea were not enough to prevent a rush of curiosity.

His room was vast. The bed was the size of a football field. There were no old-fashioned hanging lights, just the twinkle of spotlights on the ceiling. The furniture was grey, built-in, high-gloss. And, as in the sitting room, there were books and papers on surfaces. He was as casual when it came to tidiness here in his house as he was in his office. Clothes had been dumped on a chair by the window and there were two pairs of trainers on the ground, half-submerged beneath a sweatshirt.

His messiness was strangely endearing. It was almost as if he was so intensely clever, his mind so incisive and quick, that the tedious business of tidying up was a hassle he couldn't bother with. He was just too focused on other things.

She assumed he had a long-suffering housekeeper who came in and cleaned up behind him.

He was punching a number into his mobile phone, talking in a low voice, then listening to whatever was being said to him. After a handful of minutes, he disconnected the call and moved to stand by the side of the bed, arms folded.

'A few questions,' he said. 'And honest answers would be helpful.' He rattled off a series of questions and then asked finally, 'Have you eaten anything today?'

About to assure him that of course she had, Violet opened her mouth, frowned and blushed.

'Not as such...' When had she last eaten? The long trip over...the prospect of breaking the news about the pregnancy to Matt...the *stress*... Her appetite had vanished, and now she was having difficulty in remembering just what she had eaten and when.

'Not as such? What does *not as such* mean? Have you eaten anything today or not? It's a straightforward question.'

'I've been busy,' Violet mumbled.

'So when was the last time you ate?'

'Well... I picked at some food on the plane... And of course I've been meaning to pop out and do a shop... but I've been so stressed out. I think I grabbed some—'

'Stop right there, Violet. Even from the depths of my

ignorance I know that you have to have a proper eating routine when you're pregnant!' He shook his head incredulously.

'That's not fair—and it's not just because I may have missed a meal or two. I feel dizzy and nauseous a lot of the time,' she grudgingly admitted.

'We'll talk about what's fair and what's not fair once you've been fed. I'll go and…make something.' He hesitated. 'I could order something in, but I think you need to eat sooner rather than later.'

He was gone a while, during which time Violet tussled with the idea of getting out of his bed and joining him in the kitchen, but when she tried standing up she felt woozy again and had to lie back down. That being the case, the made herself as comfortable as she could. She kicked off her shoes and unbuttoned the trousers that had been a poor choice, but she had not wanted to advertise her rounded stomach any more than was necessary when it had come to confronting him with news of the pregnancy. She hadn't wanted to walk into his office and witness the look of dawning horror on his face because he had taken one look at her and guessed. No, she had wanted to build up to it because it gave her time, but she should have just worn something loose, elasticated and comfortable.

He kicked open the bedroom door and entered with a tray in his hand. 'Juice,' he said, 'and cheese on toast.' There was nothing else he could think of preparing that wouldn't have taken for ever to do.

The snack consisted of two slabs of bread lathered with butter and drowning under layers of thickly cut cheddar.

Suddenly ravenous, Violet tucked into the toast like a starving person at an all-you-can-eat buffet. Meanwhile, Matt pulled a chair to the side of the bed and watched her with narrowed eyes as she ate.

'You were telling me that your nausea wasn't solely the result of your skipping a meal or two…'

'No.'

'Let's flesh that one-syllable answer out a little, Violet. How long has this been going on?'

'From the beginning.' She fidgeted and glanced away from his all-seeing gaze. 'It's not a big deal.'

'It's a big deal. Seen the doctor about that?'

'No, of course not!' Even though she was well aware of all the problems associated with having an unplanned pregnancy—even though she was realistic enough to accept that it had hardly been her dream to have a child without the support of a caring partner by her side—the thought of going to a doctor to be told that something might go wrong filled her with dread. There had never been a moment's doubt in her mind that she very much wanted this baby.

The silence that greeted this was oppressive and forced her into speech.

'I should have eaten.' She plucked at her shirt, mouth downturned. 'I feel much better now. Lots of women suffer from extreme morning sickness. It's not a big deal, like I said. Now, I'll leave you to get on with the day and mull over everything.'

She didn't feel like leaving. She didn't fancy being on her own. She wanted to be with him when the next wave of nausea washed over her, making her want to sit down and put her head in her hands. He made her feel so safe. He was a solid brick wall, a rampart against everything that threatened to overwhelm her, and she just wanted to let him handle everything. It was silly and cowardly, but it was also an irresistible force.

'I don't think so.'

'What do you mean?'

'I mean, this business of your forgetting to eat because you've been busy has shown me that you can't be trusted to look after yourself. Don't get me wrong, I never banked on this happening, but now that it has I intend, like I said to you, to be committed the whole way through. If you can't look after yourself, then you're going to need someone to look after you, and from where I'm standing I'm the only candidate for the job.'

'It won't happen again and, if it does, I'm perfectly capable of handling it.'

'Don't fight me on this.'

Violet looked at him for a long while. She thought about the way he had reacted to news that would turn his orderly life upside down. No complaints, no accusations, no ranting and railing and tearing his hair out. No, he had risen to the occasion and had not hesitated to utter those words which for him would have been the biggest of personal sacrifices. He had proposed marriage. He didn't love her but, as he had said, he wanted to be given the chance of loving his baby on a full-time basis, and who could feel aggrieved at that?

She thought of those dark warnings as well. He was a fair guy, and she didn't think that he would really drag her through the courts to claim his rights as a father, but could she be sure? These were exceptional circumstances, and Matt Falconer was nothing if not unpredictable when it came to handling exceptional circumstances. How ruthless would he be prepared to be, and would she be able to fight him? Would she want to? Would that benefit the baby she was carrying? Her heart sped up because no one rose to the dizzy heights that he had without having his fair streak of ruthlessness.

You sometimes had to fight dirty to win wars and he'd won a lot.

'Are you threatening me?' she asked weakly.

'I seldom threaten,' Matt returned neutrally, his navy eyes never leaving her face. 'I rely on everyone else seeing sense.'

She was tempted to smile at a remark that was so typically *him*. 'I can look after myself, Matt. I've spent a lifetime doing that.'

'But was that something you chose to do, or something that circumstance chose for you?' He allowed that to sink in before continuing. 'All good things come to an end and, while you're waxing lyrical about the joys of single parenting and the nightmare of being harnessed to someone for the sake of a child, I think you should contemplate what it might feel like when you try to explain to our son or daughter down the line that they were denied the stability of two parents because you wanted to be free to find the perfect guy.'

Violet whitened. 'That's below the belt—and whoever said anything about a perfect guy?'

'And I'm very sorry that I have to bring it up, but bring it up I shall—you won't be returning to Melbourne. In your condition, long haul travel can't be a good idea.'

'You can't *kidnap* me, Matt!'

'Kidnap?' He smiled slowly and she felt that familiar warmth spread through her body, felt the tingle between her thighs that was a sharp reminder of how much power this man had over her. 'You have a very colourful image of the sort of man I'm capable of being. I draw the line at many things. Kidnapping is one of them.' He paused and their eyes locked, his stunning navy gaze pinned to her face so that even blinking felt like an effort.

'You act as though doing the right thing is somehow a crime,' Matt told her softly. 'When it comes to children, they should be put first, because they're the ones who end up bearing the scars from selfish, self-serving parents. When your father was showing me those pictures of you in his photo albums, what I saw was a guy who might have gone off the rails when it came to drink and drugs but who, when it came to the things that count, was right there. Am I wrong?'

Violet shifted uncomfortably. 'I get what you're saying, but that doesn't mean that we have to get married, Matt. We can both be here for our child even if we live apart.'

'And have separate relationships?'

'I…I hadn't thought that far ahead.' She stumbled over her words. The picture he was painting was rolling towards her with the inexorability of a tank, crushing all her fine intentions and her conviction that a union born from convenience was beyond the pale. She wanted to marry for love. What was wrong with that?

'I have no intention of letting any man bring up a child of mine,' he said bluntly. 'You can talk as much as you like about sanitised, modern caring, and sharing partnerships where all sorts of extended family members chip in, but that doesn't work for me.'

Violet shook her head in pure amazement at the tangent his thoughts had taken but, then again, Matt Falconer was not averse to dramatic exaggeration if he thought that it suited his purpose, as it did now.

That said…

Her mind drifted. What was good for the goose was good for the gander…

As if he had a direct hotline to her thoughts, he tilted his head back at a proud angle and arrowed searching eyes to her face. 'And tell me how you're going to feel if and when I find myself a doting mother figure for our child.'

'I didn't think you went for the kind of women who

doted on little kids,' Violet muttered, for want of anything better to say, and he gave an eloquent shrug of his broad shoulders.

'Needs must,' he stated succinctly. 'I would hardly be interested in continuing my current lifestyle, given the circumstances. As a father, I would want to introduce moral standards that would serve as an example to my child as he or she got older. I hadn't foreseen the necessity for getting serious with any woman but then, face it, I also hadn't foreseen that I would be in this position at this point in time.'

Violet was beginning to get a headache and the nausea was creeping up again. She lay back against the pillows and closed her eyes for a few moments.

'We can carry on this conversation at a later date,' Matt said gruffly. He turned away, and she was only aware of him talking again to the doctor he had previously called when he spun back round to face her and said without preamble, 'You're sick and my guy is coming over right now to examine you.'

'You have *a guy*?' Relief washed over her. It felt treacherously good to have someone take charge. She'd taken charge all her life. For the first time, it was great letting go! She didn't want to have any more uncomfortable conversations. She didn't want to think about that question he had posed, didn't want to project to a time when she might have to look at him with another woman— a woman wearing his ring who would be trying hard to bond with their child. 'You have a random person who drops whatever he's doing to rush over if you get a head-ache?'

Matt grinned. He relaxed, marvelled at how that quirky sense of humour could break through the clouds like a sudden, unexpected ray of sunshine. She had her eyes closed and her breathing was shallow, and the concern that ripped through him was shocking. Of course, she was having his baby, and he wouldn't have been human if he hadn't been sick with worry—because she was clearly not going to be one of those who blossomed in pregnancy—but he just wanted to reach out and smooth the strands of hair from her face.

'University friend,' he told her. 'I've done him one or two favours in the past. As it happens, this is the first time I've ever had to call upon his professional services.'

'Of course it is.'

'Never get ill. I'm as strong as an ox.'

'I don't need a doctor.'

'What you need…' Matt heard the ping of his phone announcing the arrival of his pal of old '…is to learn to depend on someone else for a change.'

Violet had to admit that it was bliss. The doctor was earnest, serious and treated Matt with the fond affection that came from many years of friendship. He was excellent at what he did, even though he was not an obstetrician but 'a brain guy', as he jokingly called himself.

'He knows everything there is to know when it comes to the human body,' Matt asserted.

'That's either a good thing,' Phillip said as he examined her with quick, efficient hands and asked pertinent questions as he did so, 'because I would clearly be a genius, or a bad thing, because a jack of all trades and master of none isn't great in an operating theatre...'

High blood pressure was the verdict. Not dangerously high, but high enough to be a cause for concern. It wouldn't be a good idea to overdo anything. Likewise, the sickness was more pronounced than usual, but not in the red zone. Combined, the young doctor declared as he headed for the bedroom door, they pointed in the direction of her having to take it easy and get a certain Matt Falconer to start discovering the joys of domesticity.

'So,' Matt drawled once he had shown his friend to the door and returned to the bedroom, 'I guess that settles the immediate question of what happens next in this scenario. It's safe to say that you won't be going anywhere any time soon...'

CHAPTER EIGHT

EVERYTHING MOVED QUICKLY after that satisfied assertion. She had been advised bed rest by a doctor, no less, and it would have been the height of irresponsibility to ignore the advice.

That had been the first arrow shot over the parapet, a warning shot of the series of persuasive arguments that were shamelessly piled on through the course of Violet's bedridden week.

'I don't want you fighting me on this,' Matt told her on more than one occasion. 'You're not interested in giving me a chance because I don't happen to live up to the mental image you have of the sort of guy you'd always dreamt of marrying, but it would be wrong to let our child pay for your scepticism.'

Violet thought back to his track record, but she knew better than to constantly remind him of it because at the back of her mind, like the promise of a storm lurking behind the illusion of clear, blue skies, was always the notion that he might fight her in court.

He'd hinted at it, and she was terrified of taking him

to task on the subject because she didn't want to hear him confirm her worst nightmare.

He had also planted a seed of treacherous unease in her head, and not only had it taken root, but it had begun to grow at an alarming rate, like the beanstalk in the fairy story. One minute there had been a harmless bean, and the next minute the bean had sprouted into a rampaging plant inhabited by fearsome creatures.

How would she feel when he began seeing another woman? That was the thought that occupied her as she remained in his sprawling apartment, ordered to stay put, her every need met either by his housekeeper, who came in daily to clean and prepare meals, or by him when he returned from work at stupidly early hours, even though she kept telling him that there was no need.

How would she find the strength to stand back and watch as another woman invested in their child?

She couldn't foresee finding another man. No one could compare to Matt, and she would never have the luxury of moving on, because he would be on her doorstep week after week, relentlessly *present*.

And in the meantime, on doctor's orders, he returned to the apartment with the regularity and perfect timing of a well-oiled Swiss watch, clumsily warming the food his housekeeper had prepared, asking her about her day, coaxing conversation out of her.

Everyone at work was asking after her, he had informed her the evening before. As soon as she was back on her feet—and that should be in the next few weeks, if Phillip was on target with his prognosis—she would have to pay them all a visit. No one could believe that he was going to be a father. She would have to show them her swelling belly to prove it.

Typically, he didn't give a hoot what his employees thought of this development and, when she had vaguely mentioned that her showing up pregnant might be some cause for embarrassment, he had burst out laughing. *Why?* he had asked with genuine curiosity. Who cared?

After a mere ten days of being treated like a china doll, Violet found that she was getting used to having him around. Indeed, she discovered that she actively and guiltily looked forward to hearing the turn of the front door handle as he entered the apartment.

Bit by bit, he was wearing down her defences and making her question the decisions she had made.

He had stopped trying to argue her into submission. Instead, he was doing it by stealth. She wondered whether it was a cunning tactic or just a method of winning that came easily to him.

The nagging thought that he was a man who wasn't made for settling down—a man who would always find temptation lurking round every corner and who would eventually be unable to resist, however dedicated a father he turned out to be—was being replaced by the dawning hope that she could somehow turn him into the guy she wanted him to be. Namely, a guy who could return her love. Given time. It happened, didn't it?

Summer was fading fast into autumn. Outside, the

days were getting shorter. She chatted to her father every day on the phone. Somehow, he had cottoned on to the fact that Matt had proposed marriage. She thought she might just come right out and ask him whether he had been having man-to-man conversations with her dad behind her back. She wouldn't put it past him.

Today, bored with languishing on a chair watching telly and reading, Violet dismissed the housekeeper and busied herself making dinner. Ever since she had moved into the apartment, the fridge had been kept in a state of readiness, well stocked with enough food to pander to her appetite whenever she might feel the need to tuck into something nutritious.

It had made her smile because the Matt she remembered when she had worked for him was a guy who had enjoyed his fast food, and she had never pictured him with a fridge containing anything but the bare essentials.

Now it was impossible to open the fridge without being bombarded by a giddying array of healthy options, from salad leaves and tomatoes to yogurt drinks awash with healthy bacteria.

She prepared a simple pasta dish, having looked up a recipe on her phone. It looked okay.

She had also done something about dressing in something other than the comfortable, loose cotton bottoms she had brought with her from Australia, and tired tee shirts which were wonderfully soft but hardly the height of glamour.

From the very moment her life had been turned on its head and she had found herself living in Matt's apartment, Violet had been determined to make sure that she kept her distance. It was unsettling enough having him around, knowing that two doors down was his bedroom, without provoking any unnecessary interest by wearing clothing that looked as though she cared.

She didn't.

Yes, she was pregnant. Yes, they had had a brief moment in time together, and so what if she was still attracted to him and he knew it? That didn't mean her head had stopped functioning. She had made her mind up, had decided that she had to detach herself from him if they were to have any sort of amicable relationship over time. They would have to learn to be friends and the way to do that was not to let her body start calling the shots.

So she had dressed down. If she'd been able to hang around in her work clothes, she would have been sorely tempted, but there was no way she could wear anything but loose-fitting clothes. Being comfortable helped the nausea, for a start.

He had gradually bought her stuff, showing up a couple of times with bags that he had casually tossed on the sofa.

'You hadn't banked on being cooped up in this apartment,' he had explained, 'And you probably hadn't banked on staying in the country for this length of time. You need more things to wear, so I got you a few things.'

He'd shrugged, headed to the kitchen for a drink and then vanished into his home office to work for a couple of hours, cutting short her protestations with an impatient wave of his hand as he'd disappeared out of sight.

Violet had taken the bags into her bedroom and inspected his offerings with indecent curiosity.

A couple were wearable. Loose silk culottes. Most weren't. They contained the right element of stretch—he'd clearly got advice from a sales assistant who had assured him that his purchases could accommodate a pregnant stomach—but the clothes were sexy, designed to draw attention, which was what she had adamantly decided not to do.

Until tonight.

Tonight, her head would no longer be in charge. The thoughts that had been turning over in her mind had borne fruit and she had come to a decision, one which left her nervous as a kitten as she waited for the sound of the door being opened.

She felt every muscle in her body clench when, at a little after seven, Matt pushed open the door to his apartment. She was waiting in the living room, standing in the doorway with a glass of juice in her hand, more to give herself something to do than because she was thirsty.

He stopped dead in his tracks and she could almost see his jaw drop in slow motion.

Which would have been hilarious if she wasn't busy trying not to feel sick.

'Am I in the right apartment?' he quipped when he had gathered some of his self-control and galvanised his legs into motion.

Eyes still on her, he dumped his leather laptop bag on the ground and shrugged off his faded, black denim jacket, which he dumped on top of the laptop bag. He slowly moved towards her, looking at her with such intensity that she knew her skin was turning bright red. Matching the stretchy dress she had chosen to wear. One of the inappropriate items she had foreseen would hit the back of the wardrobe, never to see the light of day again.

Until she'd decided that it would be tonight's statement piece because a big decision warranted something more dramatic than jogging bottoms and a tee shirt.

'I've cooked.' Violet cleared her throat, eyes skittering away the closer he got, until he was so close that she could smell the woody scent of his aftershave.

'You've cooked,' Matt murmured, his breath a feathery caress against her burning skin. 'What happened to Marita? Did you stuff her in a cupboard somewhere because her soufflé wasn't up to scratch?'

His voice was a warm caress and her skin burned in response. Now that she had come to a decision, she allowed her mind to wander into all sorts of previously forbidden terrain… Lying in bed next to him, his touch, the low, silky murmur of his voice, the strength of his arms wrapped around her. The thought of just being able to drop her guard and laugh at his sense of humour.

Only now did she realise how exhausting it had been, keeping up her defences, not allowing herself to fully relax because she'd been so scared that if she took her eye off the ball she would cave in.

All those thoughts he had generated in her head… that beanstalk that had seemingly sprung up overnight… It no longer felt like caving in. It felt like an inevitable outcome and she wasn't sure whether he had deliberately engineered that or not.

'I'm feeling so much better.' She tilted her head to look at him. He was so stupidly good-looking, she thought. All sexy alpha male with a sense of humour that could pull a smile from a block of ice.

'Does that account for the change of outfit as well?' His voice was lazy and curious but his eyes were serious with intent.

'Do you like it?'

Matt stilled. His eyes never left her face. 'I've either done something wrong or else you're about to tell me something I won't be interested in hearing. Which will it be?'

'I do want to have a talk with you,' Violet admitted, turning away because she could no longer bear the intensity of his gaze. 'Maybe we should sit.' She led the way to the low leather sofa and he followed her. She noted that he made sure to keep his distance, sitting on one of the chairs instead of on the sofa next to her.

'Well,' he drawled after a moment's silence, during which Violet tried to get her thoughts into some kind of chronological order, 'are you going to spit it out or will we have a protracted guessing game?'

'I've been thinking,' Violet began, hesitantly. He had proposed marriage once upon what felt like a long time ago, but since then he had taken a back seat, and now she wondered whether he hadn't had a rethink. Had he had time seriously to weigh up the pros and cons of settling down with her? Had close proximity over the past week and a half made him realise that having her around was really too much of an acquired taste?

She thought of all the blondes who had cluttered his life. Had enforced time spent with her made him realise that he missed that type of woman? He'd never had to tailor his work schedule to accommodate any of them and, while it was one thing waxing lyrical about doing the right thing for the sake of the baby she was carrying, it was another thing altogether when he was put to the test and actually had to make sacrifices.

She knew that he was often up when she retired to her bedroom because she was so finely tuned to the pad of his steps on the wooden landing. Two mornings ago, she had woken up to use the bathroom and she had heard him walk past her door, his footsteps barely audible. It had been two thirty in the morning. For a man who had always enjoyed complete freedom of movement, who had become accustomed to dating women who never interfered with whatever routines he had in place, he had now been put to the test, and she did wonder whether it was proving an eye-opener for him.

All those thoughts nearly made her immediately start the process of backtracking, but then she thought of him with another woman sometime in the future... Coming by to collect their child... Zooming off in one of those fast cars of his so that he and whomever he happened to be dating could have a bonding weekend...

'You've been thinking,' Matt prompted. 'Going to share any of those thoughts this side of Christmas? Because I'm all ears.'

'I'll admit that when I found out about the baby...' she hesitated and frowned, thinking back to what seemed ages ago '...I wasn't sure what your reaction was going to be. I know you were furious when I told you that I'd considered not saying anything at all, but you have to understand that I know you very well.'

'A little knowledge can be a dangerous thing,' Matt murmured. 'It can lead to all sorts of misinformed conclusions.'

'Well, yes. But, at any rate, I don't think I would have withheld the information from you. You had to know, you had to be given the choice of what you wanted to do. It helped that I had my own source of income and you knew that there was no way you could use your money to control the situation.'

Matt's eyebrows shot up and he stared at her.

'You know what I'm talking about, Matt,' Violet told him drily, 'so don't even think of playing the innocent with me. If I'd been broke, you would have used your wealth to get me to do what you wanted and I wouldn't have had much choice.'

'That's a terrible accusation.' But there was a ghost of a smile on his face as he continued to look at her from under lowered lashes.

'You did make me think when you hinted that you would consider taking me to court, however.'

The smile dropped from his face instantly. 'It was a vague threat that I would never have gone through with.'

'And it was a chance I couldn't take.'

'I would like to tell you, right here and right now, that no decision of yours should be based on any apprehension on your part that I might fight you in a court of law for custody of this baby. It would never happen. If I insinuated otherwise, well, you know my nature, Violet. I'm a man accustomed to fighting the good fight when it comes to getting what I want.'

Violet shrugged. 'Living here with you,' she said slowly, 'has made me realise that you might actually mean it when you say that you would be prepared to do whatever it takes for the sake of this baby. You've gone beyond the call of duty when it came to...to taking care of me. That was something you hadn't banked on and you rose to the occasion.'

'Thank you for the sweeping compliment, Violet, but it's fair to say that Marita did pull her weight. Had you had to rely on my culinary skills, you probably wouldn't be sitting here being quite so effusive in your praise.'

But he was still wary of what she was about to say.

Violet could sense that underneath the easy charm and the lazy banter. She knew the way his mind worked. He would be predicting, forecasting, mentally trying to piece together a puzzle that was still missing a few parts. Matt Falconer was a guy who was always a dozen steps ahead of everyone else. It occurred to her that she had turned that routine firmly on its head and she marvelled that he had gone with the flow instead of trying to fight against the current.

'You told me that I was being selfish when I rejected your proposal of marriage. For my part, all I wanted for myself was a conventional marriage with someone who chose to spend his life with me instead of a guy forced into it because of circumstances. So I turned you down...'

'And now?' He tilted his head to one side, giving nothing away.

'And now... Well, this is about more than what I want and what I expected from life. I can't deny this baby the right to both parents and a stable background. So...'

'So...? I book the church and buy the ring?'

If there was one giveaway that this was a marriage of convenience and not something he truly wanted, it was wrapped up in that amused quip. Her heart constricted. Was she doing the right thing? Yes, she thought. She was. Because, if her heart tightened now, then the thought of what the alternative was made it tighten even more painfully.

'Not quite,' she told him quietly. 'There's no need to

do either of those things just yet. I suggest…we continue living together. See how things progress. I'm getting stronger by the day. Let's take it a step at a time. We can always reassess further down the road.'

For a few moments there was silence, then he said with just the smallest of shrugs, 'In that case, I think step number one should be meeting the parents…'

It couldn't be avoided. Matt knew that. Whatever the state of play between him and his parents, they had to be in the loop, and who knew? They might have held him at a distance—stiffly, silently and permanently dis-approving, disappointed at the direction he had chosen for himself—but maybe, just maybe, what they hadn't been able to show him, they might be able to show their grandchild.

It felt like a terrifyingly huge step. That didn't mean that he could, or even wanted to, shy away from it…

Violet looked at her reflection in the mirror with trou-bled eyes. She'd foolishly thought that everything would somehow slot into place after that talk but now, three days later, she was still unsure as to what was going on.

He hadn't scooped her into his arms and swept her up to his bedroom, which she had kind of hoped he would. Instead, they had had a very sensible conversation about what happened next. Yes, the parents. She would have to meet them. Despite the fact that the whole world seemed to know about the baby, he still hadn't broken the news to them, and when she'd shown surprise, he had simply averted his eyes and told her that it was the sort of conversation that had to be had face-to-face and he just hadn't had time to make the trip.

They had discussed the need to move out of London. His apartment was enormous, but it was essentially a bachelor pad. Glass, metal and grey furniture didn't add up to a child-friendly environment.

She had felt uncomfortably out of place in the sexy red dress, because what she had imagined might turn into something a little seductive had actually ended up with the feel of a board meeting. She hadn't really understood what was going on, and she wondered whether his interpretation of her living with him to see how things went, as opposed to marrying him, meant simply a continuation of what they already had. A perfectly civilised relationship in which she inhabited one of the spare rooms, except maybe the spare room would be in a house outside London instead of an apartment in the centre.

She had slept on her own that night, as she had previously, and he had then vanished to New York for an urgent meeting he couldn't afford to skip.

Now, here they were. He would be back from the airport any minute. He'd called and told her that he was en route. That they would then leave immediately for the meet-the-parents visit.

'Don't you want to have a breather after a long-haul flight?' she had asked dubiously, but no, he didn't need a breather, he had told her. Only wimps needed breathers.

His parents were expecting him and there was no opt-out clause there.

So here she was, dressed in an outfit that brokered a deal between sensible and a little daring, because she had no real idea what his parents were like. The dress was black, long-sleeved and showed off her now visible bump, but in a way that was still prim and proper even though the dress was reasonably fitted.

She was wearing thick, black tights and her hair was neatly tucked behind her ears. She felt like the PA she had once been.

She was dressed and anxiously waiting when she heard the sound of the front door opening, and she couldn't contain the surge of high-wire tension and excitement that raced through her.

He was in a pair of faded jeans, a black sweater and a beaten leather jacket. And *still* he managed to look effortlessly cool and ridiculously elegant.

Their eyes met and for a few seconds neither said anything, then Matt lowered his eyes and said, huskily, 'You're ready. You look great, Violet.'

He hesitated.

He wanted to move towards her and take her in his arms, but he remained hovering for a few seconds, wondering how it was that she had opened the door between them and yet, more than ever before in his life, he was afflicted with a sense of uncertainty that he didn't quite know how to deal with. She exerted a spell over him. He could feel himself wanting to get closer, wanting to sink into her, and that weakness confused him but still it was there, persistent and ever-present.

He knew that she would have been bewildered at his behaviour. No sooner had she told him that she wanted to try to work things out between them as a couple, as a united team for the sake of their baby, than he had disappeared across the Atlantic, leaving her on her own.

He could barely formulate a coherent explanation to give her, but he knew that he would have to, and soon. Today.

He would have to have that talk with her, tell her that he could never love her, that she should banish any such hopes from her head, if they were indeed there at all.

This would be an arrangement, and a very successful one if she didn't fall into the trap of expecting more than would ever be on offer. There could be no other conversation on the subject. He didn't do love, he didn't know *how* to…and if it sometimes felt as though she might be the one, might occupy a space he had never carved out in his heart, well, he would slam the door on those seditious thoughts.

He hadn't laid a finger on her, and it was driving him nuts, but the speech had to be delivered before any other roads were taken.

He restlessly raked his fingers through his hair and thought that he had never, in his entire life, seen a sight as beautiful as the woman standing uncertainly in front of him, her hand resting lightly on her small bump.

'Would you like something to eat? Drink?' Violet asked hesitantly, and he smiled.

'It's six thirty. Something will be laid on,' he commented drily. 'It's an hour to their house. The sooner we get there, the better.'

'Tell me what I should be expecting,' Violet prodded when they were in the car and powering out of London towards Surrey, leaving the cluttered streets behind.

She couldn't tear her eyes away from his face. She wanted so much to do something simple and intimate— place her hand on his thigh, feel the ripple of muscle— but the weird distance he had created between them made her cautious.

She so wanted to ask him outright if he had gone off her. Pregnancy, as it progressed, was not that appealing to lots of guys. Was he one of them? One of those men who were ever so vaguely repulsed by the sight of an expanding stomach?

Maybe he had got it into his head that she was off limits because the doctor had advised rest.

Violet had no idea how to broach the thorny issue, but surely they couldn't work as a couple if they still carried on occupying separate bedrooms?

They made amicable conversation as the fast car ate up the miles, speeding to a destination that turned out to be nothing at all like what she had expected.

They had gone from the congested streets of London into open spaces where ribbons of houses were crammed along narrow roads, punctuated with traffic lights, pedestrians and cars. London on a smaller scale. But then that had been left behind, giving way to grander properties enclosed in land and guarded by gates. The car continued to bypass the grander houses until it turned left and they were confronted with the sort of impressive wrought-iron gates that advertised barking guard dogs, CCTV cameras and someone on patrol to keep intruders out.

Violet's mouth dropped open.

'This is where your parents live?'

'Your average mansion.' Matt shrugged and used a beeper on his key ring to open the gates.

'Wow. It's not exactly a four-bedroomed semi on an estate, is it…?' She glanced across at him and frowned, because his body language shrieked tension. His jaw was clenched and his fingers were tightly gripping the steering wheel.

'When was the last time you saw your parents?' she asked, her attention diverted by the tree-shaded drive that wound its way towards… Well, this was beyond a mansion. This was something along the lines of a National Trust estate. She gaped, not because she wasn't used to big houses and over-the-top mansions, many of which she had experienced first-hand over the years with her dad, but because this was just so…unexpected. She tried hard to quench a sickening rush of acute nerves while he briefly informed her that he visited four times a year.

'Exactly four times?' Her mouth felt dry, which was

the opposite of the palms of her hands, which were clammy. This felt like a really big deal, a turning point in a relationship that had been pleasantly meandering along, somehow waiting for something to happen.

'Three birthdays and Christmas day.'

'That's very organised.' She looked across at him. 'I didn't think you were that organised a person.'

'When you meet my parents, you'll discover why organisation is important. They're not people who appreciate spontaneous drop-ins.'

The rolling mansion drew closer. It was an impressive but grim edifice of greystone, fronted with a circular courtyard dominated by an amazing fountain. On either side of the house, sprawling, well-manicured lawns rolled off towards the dark shadows of trees.

'Don't worry.' He turned to her wryly when he'd killed the engine. 'It won't be a protracted visit.'

She was struck by a sudden thought. 'Have you told them that I am going to be with you?'

'Like I said, I preferred the face-to-face approach.'

'They're going to be shocked.'

'Maybe they will.'

'Don't you care? You've put me in an awful position!'

'I wouldn't worry about it.' He looked at her for a few seconds, then eased himself out of the car, moving round to open the passenger door for her.

'Of course I'm worried! Most parents love all the excitement of their child announcing that a baby's on the way! They're going to be so disappointed.'

Matt laughed humourlessly. 'Like I said, Violet, don't worry about it. When it comes to disappointment, there are no surprises in store. I've been living with it all of my life.'

CHAPTER NINE

AFTERWARDS, VIOLET THOUGHT that she should have pieced together something of what she would find from that remark.

A man who can indifferently reflect that parental disappointment has been his lot in life would not be a man to enjoy a warm relationship with his parents, and they could not have been less like the fun-loving, outgoing people she had always assumed they would be.

Not that she had ever had any clues to go on because, although he was ridiculously open when it came to the women in his life and the chaotic revolving door of his relationships, he had always been tight-mouthed about his background.

She certainly had not expected them to be made of money, but they were. The front door was opened by a butler—butlers still existed!—and they were shown into a sitting room the size of an airfield.

To look at, Lord and Lady Falconer made an impressively good-looking couple. She was tall and elegant, with luxurious dark hair firmly pulled back. Traces of a Spanish heritage could be seen in her colouring, the slightly olive-toned skin and the dark eyes.

He, likewise, was tall and distinguished, the absolute epitome of an English gentleman, from the way he carried himself to the suit and tie he wore.

Violet had no idea how old they were. Certainly in their midsixties. But their mannerisms, their strained formality, made them seem much older.

Conversation was polite. Violet cringed when his mother's eyes flicked over her stomach but Matt introduced the topic without the slightest hint of embarrassment or apology. Both parents nodded their congratulations and asked precious few questions.

Accustomed as she was to a life filled with exuberant, over-the-top adults, Violet was bewildered and, after an hour of stilted conversation, deeply saddened for Matt and a childhood that had obviously been quite different from her own. Perhaps, had he not been an only child, things might have been a little better. Violet could only shudder at the thought of a young child, packed off to boarding school at the age of seven, spending holidays and free time in a house that had the feel of a mausoleum.

More than ever, she felt *special* to have been introduced to his parents. She was quite sure that he had never allowed any overlap between his parents and his women. Yes, she was pregnant, and that made a big difference, but nothing could take away from the fact that it felt like a significant step.

Dinner was served in the dining room, where they all attempted conversation across a table so vast that megaphones wouldn't have been a bad idea.

The food was delicious. Four courses, with all the appropriate wines, although neither of them had anything to drink. She was pregnant, and Matt was insistent on driving back—even though, as an afterthought, his mother did mention that a room could be prepared for them and the drive undertaken in the morning.

'Work,' Matt informed them with a polite smile, glancing at his watch, which seemed to be an accepted signal as both parents rose without fuss, leaving the dishes to be cleared away by the invisible young girl who had ferried them in.

'Coffee in the snug?' his father asked. 'Or something stronger? I have some excellent port.'

'I have a stack of emails to get through before morning,' Matt informed them both and, whilst neither parent said anything, Violet noticed the fleeting moue of distaste that had crossed his father's face. Then they were at the front door, with coats being brought to them and congratulations repeated on the pregnancy.

'We must lunch,' his mother said politely. 'I visit London every so often and I would be delighted to take you somewhere.'

Violet nodded and wondered how that would go. Lunch with Julietta Falconer? The conversation would not flow, that was for sure.

'I told you it wouldn't be a protracted affair,' was

the first thing Matt said once they were in the car and heading away from the country estate.

'Do you normally have such…formal meals with your parents?'

Matt slung her a sideways glance. 'They're not the sort who enjoy casual dining round a kitchen table.'

'I never knew… I wasn't expecting…'

'I prefer not to dwell on my background. I find it muddies the water.'

'Was it always like that?'

He shrugged. 'Boarding school broke it up.' He paused and said neutrally, eyes fixed on the road ahead, making brilliant time in the darkness on the empty country lanes, 'I envy the chaotic life you must have led, Violet, even though you probably might have wished it could have been different when you were growing up.'

'I always felt that there was so much responsibility on my shoulders. Without a mother and with my dad and his carefree lack of self-control—you're right. I used to long for a bit of stability.'

'Which is why you reacted by becoming the very antithesis of your father. Where he was wild, you were grounded. You looked out for him and, in the process, you sacrificed the sort of life most young girls would have led.'

'This is a pretty deep conversation to be having so late in the evening.'

Matt smiled crookedly. 'Sometimes deep conversations are called for. I don't usually do them but, hey, there are exceptions to every rule.'

Violet glanced across at him with uneasy eyes, sensing that he wanted to say something she might not be overjoyed to hear, but really not sure what that something might be.

But that glimpse into his past had made her hungry for more, and curiosity was a greater force than wariness.

'Your parents don't approve of what you do, do they?'

'What makes you say that?' Startled, Matt slid his gaze across to her, eyes narrowed.

'Just a feeling I got.'

'Explain.'

'There was something in your dad's expression when you told him that we had to leave because you had work to do when you got back to London.'

Bitterness crept into Matt's voice when he next spoke. 'My destiny was to manage that sprawling estate and, for fun, have a career in the city or at the very least at the bar. Something traditional and respectable. Along with marriage to the right girl with the right connections.'

'They told you that?'

'Not in so many words,' Matt said drily. 'But, then again, meaningful conversation has always been thin on the ground. The chosen way has always been to circle around what needed to be said aloud.'

Hence, Violet thought, his remark about being a disappointment. Her heart went out to him. What must he have felt growing up? He was now the biggest success story in the tech industry but, as far as his parents were concerned, he was a let down, pursuing a career they probably didn't fully understand and maybe disapproved of.

'I can hear the sound of you feeling sorry for me,' he continued.

'Of course I do.' She reached out, rested her hand on his arm and felt him stiffen fractionally. In response, she whipped her hand away, cheeks red.

'Matt.' She sighed with exasperation. 'You should tell me what's going on. I thought…' She breathed in deeply and ploughed on, because nothing felt right at the moment. 'I thought that when I agreed to give our relationship a go you might have been a little more enthusiastic, especially considering you were the one to suggest… Well, you asked me to marry you and I turned you down. Now I'm prepared to meet you halfway but I get the feeling that you're not at all overjoyed with the situation. You vanished like a bat out of hell the second I told you that I was prepared to give things a go and now you can barely look me in the face. Meeting your parents…felt like a big step forward, but was it? Or was it just a hurdle that had to be jumped?'

'You deserve to have all those questions answered,' he said roughly.

Violet felt a chill run through her. How had she managed to misjudge the situation so badly? He'd been the perfect partner when he had had no choice but to take care of her, but while he had been fetching and carrying and making sure that her feet were up and she was getting the bed rest the doctor had recommended, he had had time and opportunity to consider his options.

He liked her and she was his responsibility and, whilst that combination had initially propelled him into that rash marriage proposal, things had changed. He had backed away from that drastic suggestion and now saw things the way she had. Standing back at a distance, he had doubtless come to appreciate that they could have a perfectly amicable relationship without him committing to putting a ring on her finger.

Maybe, just maybe, he had even begun casting his net out there. Maybe, just maybe, he had realised that he could have her as a friend and carry on with his Lothario ways. How many men didn't want to have their cake and eat it? Bit by bit, she had thawed and pushed past her inherent fears that he wouldn't turn out to be the dependable guy she needed, that he *couldn't* be that person. Had she made a terrible mistake?

'What are you doing?' she asked, dismayed, as he swung off the main road, heading down a side street signposting a village, a place she had never heard of.

'We need to talk and I don't want to talk in the car. I can't focus on the road and the conversation we have to have.'

'Then let's wait until we're back in London.' Violet was only now appreciating just how much she had come to rely on him and just how far she had taken it for granted that he would be thrilled were she to give ground and do what he had wanted her to do when she had first broken the news of her pregnancy. Mistakes and misjudgements all round, it would seem.

Matt didn't answer. He seemed to know this part of the world well, considering his visits to his parents were confined to four times a year, but then he would have grown up in these parts, maybe wanting to escape the claustrophobia of his ancestral home as soon as he was old enough to do so.

Very quickly, they pulled up to a brightly lit pub. The car park was full but they managed to squeeze into a space and then, without exchanging conversation, they headed inside, where he was greeted by the landlord like an old buddy.

They found a bench seat at the back by one of only the few tables. It was a little after ten but the place was still busy.

Matt went up to the bar and returned with two drinks, something alcoholic for him and a glass of elderflower for her.

'It's late,' he said gruffly. 'There are nice rooms upstairs. I've booked us in for the night.'

'Why?'

'Because I want a drink, and I don't do drinking and driving. Now that you've met my parents, Violet, you can maybe see…why my approach to relationships is somewhat, shall we say, different to yours. You long for stability. You've lived your life pursuing the dream of finding the perfect partner and settling down.' He took one long mouthful of whisky and sat back to look at her. 'I, Violet, have not.'

'No,' Violet said quietly. 'I get that now.'

'Tell me what you get.'

'You never felt loved, at least not loved in the way most people acknowledge it—nothing verbal, nothing tactile,' she ventured tentatively. 'And if someone has never felt loved, then how do they know how to love? You've never done long-term relationships because you've never seen the point of them. In your world, there's no such thing as love, so why would you encourage any woman to look in that direction if you know that you can't deliver. Am I right?'

She thought of his parents, their oppressive lack of emotion. She thought of the hopes she had nurtured of him loving her the way she loved him. Those hopes were slowly evaporating like mist on a hot summer morning. 'You've had time to think things through and you've realised that you can't settle down to any kind of relationship with me, even though you probably wish you could, because like you said, you have dreams of being a full-time father.'

Violet forced herself to smile. It made her face ache. 'Of course, you're right, and I don't know what I was thinking when I said that I was prepared to give things a go. It's all working perfectly well between us as it stands! I'm more or less back on my feet as well, so I should be out of your hair very soon.'

He was frowning and Violet banked down a surge of impatience. Was she being obtuse? She didn't think so!

'What makes you think that I'm no longer interested in marrying you?'

'B-because…!' Violet spluttered. 'Because I can *tell*.'

'Really? How?'

'You act as though I've suddenly become a stranger,' she muttered under her breath, hating him for directing the conversation down this uncomfortable road.

'How do you want me to act?'

'This is a ridiculous conversation,' Violet said sharply. 'I know the lie of the land, Matt. That's the main thing.'

'I've been distant because I didn't want you to get any unrealistic ideas, should we embark on a full-time relationship.'

'What are you talking about?' Her voice had cooled and her brown eyes were wary and remote.

'Things felt…comfortable, Violet. The way we slipped into a routine.' He lowered his gaze, very much aware that he, too, had become disturbingly accustomed to the routine they had established.

'And you thought that, because there was some kind of routine, I might start pining over what was never going to be on the table.'

'I'm not a man who knows how to love. It's the way I'm built. Can you live with that?'

Violet shrugged but inside something had broken. Could she live with this guy, knowing that he would never love her the way she wanted him to? He was nothing if not honest and he was giving her an opt-out clause. She thought of him moving on and felt faint.

'Like you said at the beginning, Matt, this isn't just about us. This is about a baby who didn't ask to be conceived and about giving this baby of ours the best chance in life. Sacrifices have to be made. What we have is good just the way it is… And if it's not exactly what I had in mind for myself, then that's life. It's all about compromise.'

He was looking at her carefully. 'I've booked us into separate rooms.'

'Have you?'

'I had no idea how this conversation would go.'

'And now?'

'You tell me, Violet.'

'It's stupid to think that we can try to make a go of this without…without…'

Matt smiled, a slow, curling smile that made her pulse race.

'I'll let them know that we'll only need one room, shall I?'

The exhaustion that had wiped her out when she had been at his parents' house faded fast as they finished their drinks and made their way up to a charming, tiny bedroom with old-fashioned chintz curtains and a matching bedspread on the double bed. She felt as nervous as a kitten, and it almost made her laugh when she thought that she was carrying this man's baby, so nerves should have been the last thing she felt as she watched him get undressed, his movements slow and casual, his eyes focused on her the whole time.

'You have no idea how much I've missed this, Violet. Watching you…watching you grow…knowing that I shouldn't touch.'

He stepped towards her, naked and erect, and warmth flooded her. She crept into his arms as easily as if she belonged there and rested her head against his chest.

'I've missed it as well,' she responded gruffly, talking into his chest. He gently held her at arm's length and looked at her.

'Important question. Is this okay for the baby?'

Violet laughed. 'Of course it is!'

'Good. I'd googled, out of curiosity, but who believes what they read on a computer screen?'

'Ninety-nine percent of the population?'

Matt smiled and flushed. 'I've missed more than the sex, if I'm honest. I've missed your sense of humour.' He swept her off her feet, took her to the bed and then stood to look down at her. Violet couldn't help herself. She reached out and touched him and hot moisture pooled between her legs as his erect manhood pulsed against the slow, feathery brush of her finger.

Very slowly she touched him the way she knew he liked being touched, firm and slow, and he arched back, breathing quickening as lazily she continued to arouse him, then she straddled the side of the bed, her legs apart, and licked the rigid length of his shaft. She let her hands drop to caress the sensitive skin of his inner thighs and he groaned and curled his fingers into her hair, directing her mouth. He finally drew her away with a shudder.

'No way are you going to take me there with your mouth,' he chastised her in a roughened undertone and she grinned back at him.

This felt so good, so right—as though they were meant to be with one another. She locked seditious thoughts away, thoughts of the impossible. He had set her straight on how he felt and, having met his parents, she could see how he had ended up as he had, the key to his heart thrown out like so much useless garbage. But they would be together and, if this was second best, then she would accept that.

She began undressing and desire bloomed even more because he was watching her with that way he had, focused and intense, as though even her slightest movements were a source of fascination for him.

He helped her, in the end. He couldn't resist. Her clothes joined his on the ground and they managed to rid the bed of the chintz spread, laughing as they peeled it back while trying to hold one another at the same time. That, too, ended up in a crumpled bundle on the ground.

She was naked and it felt liberating.

He reverently stroked her swollen stomach.

'Your breasts have grown,' he murmured. 'I'd wondered. Fantasised. Having you share the apartment with me was a test of willpower I never knew I possessed. So don't try to stop me from exploring every inch of your body now.'

'I wouldn't dream of it.'

He curved his hand to cup a breast and held it as though weighing it up for size, then he rolled the pad of his thumb over her nipple and felt it stiffen under his finger.

Her breasts had grown, as had her nipples, which had darkened into big, circular discs.

One touch and Matt knew that he wouldn't be able to steel himself from coming in an undignified premature ejaculation. He closed his eyes and nuzzled the softness of her breasts, eliciting little whimpers of pleasure, then he suckled on her nipple, teasing the stiffened tip with his tongue and simultaneously curving his hand between her thighs so that he could feel the dampness between her legs.

She relaxed against the pressure of his hand there. She arched back in a gesture that was gratifyingly and seductively submissive. Submission wasn't something she did and her unconscious desire to yield to him was a massive turn-on.

The swell of her stomach was a massive turn-on as well.

He nudged into her gently, levering himself in just the perfect position to appreciate her. He moved slowly and firmly, taking his time and gritting his teeth because he wanted to do just the opposite, but, God, he wanted to make this last. It felt as if it had been a long time coming.

Violet succumbed to the surge of indescribable pleasure as one gentle thrust almost took her over the edge. She clung to him and wrapped her legs around his waist. Like this, in the heat of the moment, she could sneak a glance at his face. His eyes were glazed with desire as he pushed into her. He wasn't registering her and, for a few seconds, she could luxuriate in looking at him with absolute love.

Forbidden love. She closed her eyes and inhaled sharply as sensation spiralled, wiping out frustrating thoughts. He was moving faster now, his thrusts deeper and, oh, so satisfying. It had been a long time. It felt like years.

She came with an intensity that shocked her, her body trembling as wave upon wave of pure sensation rocked her with the force of a tsunami.

She clasped his muscled back, her fingers digging into his bronzed skin. She doubted he was aware of anything, though. He was arched up, his eyes closed, nostrils slightly flared as he found his own powerful release, swearing aloud as he orgasmed inside her. She could feel his fluid rush into her body, and for a few seconds she thought of the baby they had created when they had made love that first time without any protection.

The love she felt for him was so strong, her breath caught in her throat. She wanted to pull him close to her but then, almost immediately, she acknowledged the foolishness of her feelings because she, of all the people in the world, should know him for the man that he was. She had dispatched enough farewell bouquets of flowers on his behalf! Heck, she had the local Knightsbridge florist he used on speed dial!

She'd just never really worked out how how deep his cynicism ran. Now she knew.

They curved towards one another and he smiled, hand on her stomach.

'I never thought I'd enjoy saying this to a woman, but let's make plans.'

'Okay.' She paused. They were a couple and this was as good as it got with him. There had to be a certain businesslike approach to the situation or else it would run away with her and she didn't want that. 'But first, there's something we should get straight between us.'

'What's that?'

'This has to be a…monogamous relationship. If we're a couple, then no fooling around.'

Matt propped himself up on one elbow and looked at her with interest. 'I thought that monogamy was reserved for faithfully married couples,' he murmured. 'Love, cherish, honour, et cetera, et cetera…'

'But we're missing those qualities, aren't we?' Violet quipped, lowering her eyes to shield the hurt she was certain he would be able to glimpse, even though it was dark in the bedroom and he would have needed bionic vision to read what she was thinking.

'I'm a one-woman man, Violet,' he gently repri-
manded her.

'Even though we're not a faithfully married couple?'

'You could always rectify that.'

Temptation loomed. What was the big difference between living together and being married? Violet knew
that it should have been a case of, in for a penny, in for a
pound, but somehow marriage felt like a huge step. She
would be accepting, without hope of retraction, a situation that she knew was barely acceptable. She would
be signing away her future because a little of this man
was better than nothing at all. Except what if, one day,
she began to think otherwise? Then what? She couldn't
think of the hassle and hopelessness of divorce without
her blood running cold.

At least, living together, she could cling to the illusion that there was a way out if things became truly
unbearable.

'It's more sensible for us to see how things work
out between us.' She dug her heels in and stared at the
bronzed, flat planes of his chest. She felt him shrug,
then he lay back and stared up at the ceiling.

'Sensible,' he murmured under his breath. 'It's what
I've always admired about you. When everyone's losing their heads...'

That stung. Was that still what he thought of her deep
down? That she was his practical, sensible secretary
who could be relied upon to steer a steady ship when
the rest of the world seemed to be going mad? Hadn't

he got past that by now? If he hadn't, then it really was for the best that they weren't about to tie any knots any time soon, because the joys of a common-sense wife would wear very thin very fast.

But without a ring on her finger…without the status of *wife*…would his loyalty be something she could ever take for granted?

Violet realised that if she gave house room to all those niggling doubts at the back of her mind, then she would never be free of them, and if she were to stick to her word and really give this relationship a chance, at least to see whether she could actually take the crumbs and forfeit the loaf of bread, then she would have to forge past misgivings.

She rested her hand on his stomach. 'The sensible thing, right now, would be to discuss what happens next. I mean, the nuts and bolts of it. My dad seems to be coming round to the idea of returning here to live. I think he's energised by the thought of having a grandchild. Anyway, he's talking about using the music school he started in Melbourne as a template for doing something similar over here. Not in London. I think he's learned to appreciate a slower lane, living out there.'

'I'm not sure I'm in the mood for talking about sensible things just at the moment,' Matt drawled, flattening his hand over hers and then directing it to where his libido was, once more, making itself felt. 'Let's make up for lost time and throw sensible to the winds…just for tonight.'

* * *

Everything, over the next two months, seemed to move at a very slow pace. Matt would not let her do anything he felt might be a set back to her health, even though she had long since been given the all-clear by the obstetrician she had been assigned by the private hospital he'd insisted on. Having rapidly decided that a move out of London was essential, and having discussed in record time where that somewhere might be—ideally allowing a commute into London without sacrificing the country lifestyle they both agreed would be a good choice for a family—it was frustrating that house viewings were confined to when Matt was free, because he flatly refused to let Violet get wrapped up in the stress of house hunting on her own.

She could look at brochures, he told her as they idly lay in bed one Sunday morning, flicking through houses online. Looking at brochures would be good for her blood pressure. She reminded him that her blood pressure was fine, but lying there naked, her leg loosely over his, she had never been happier.

This felt like what being a couple was all about. Time was moving on and, if the whole subject of marriage had gone onto the back burner, then it was because they were both enjoying what they had. So why complicate matters by rocking the boat?

She was luxuriating in all sorts of taboo thoughts about love, happy-ever-afters, and other never-to-be-tabled scenarios, when she heard the buzz of her mobile.

It was a little after six in the evening. Outside, night had fallen and there was a glacial chill to the air that was a reminder that winter was lurking just round the corner. Inside the apartment, Violet was already in her comfy clothes. Bedroom slippers, jogging bottoms and a loose tee shirt, over which she was wearing a hand-me-down cardigan from her father who, as he had grown older, had adopted a curiously traditional sartorial style.

Slouching around was exactly what she would be doing for the next three days because Matt was in New York. As he had been the previous month, although only for two nights. He'd explained the deal to her, but her brain had been fuzzy, and he had burst out laughing when she'd yawned halfway through the details about an app that could do clever things involving personal finance. Not as amusing as the games industry, Matt had said, but anything to keep body and soul together—which was rich, coming from a billionaire.

It took her a few seconds to register the female voice down the end of the line and, even when she did, her first reaction was puzzlement more than anything else.

'Glo?' She parroted the name and then, just for added confirmation, 'Glo Bale from the flower shop?'

'The very same.' Glo laughed.

She was a middle-aged woman with a bubbly personality and an infectious laugh. She and Violet had exchanged many a coded conversation in the past about Matt's predilection for goodbye bouquets without once overstepping the line. It was a telephone relationship that had always been comfortable and amicable.

'I'm sorry to bother you, my darling,' Glo said breathlessly, 'but I've been trying to get through to your lovely boss...'

Ex-boss, Violet thought absently. Clearly, Glo was not in the loop and she wondered what the other woman would think.

'He's away at the moment. New York.'

'Probably busy in meetings,' Glo said. 'But here's the thing. He left a message for me to prepare one of his bouquets. Said he'd get back to me to confirm details, but I haven't heard, and the flowers are going to begin heading for the big botanical garden in the sky if he doesn't get his skates on and fill me in on the details.'

'A—a bouquet?' Violet stammered.

'Over-the-top one, if I'm honest, my darling.'

'Over-the-top...' She cleared her throat. Her stomach was doing weird things, freewheeling, making her feel giddy and sick. 'Thanks for calling, Glo. I'll... I'll tell him to get in touch with you... Thanks.'

She hung up and stared sightlessly at her mobile.

Flowers? A bouquet? Over-the-top?

Who was he saying goodbye to?

CHAPTER TEN

Missed your calls. Sorry. Been busy.

SIX WORDS. BUT the minute Matt read them on his mobile he knew that something was seriously wrong. He just couldn't figure out what that something might be, because up until then life had been going swimmingly, for want of a better word.

He had one more day left. New York was less than its usual invigorating self and he couldn't focus. What was that text message supposed to mean?

The meeting room on the fifty-ninth floor of a skyscraper that had topped the charts for creativity felt stifling. There were dozens of people milling around, almost as though there was no deal to be done, and they had all the time in the world to talk about nothing in particular while guzzling limitless glasses of champagne.

When Matt looked around him, he couldn't see an end to the deal that, yet again, would amass millions in the years to come. The only thing he could see were those cool, impersonal words on his mobile, a response to the unanswered phone calls and text messages.

Been busy. *Doing what?*

Yes, she was back on her feet. Her blood pressure had stabilised. The sickness had gone. Of course, he thought distractedly, she was busy because she was no longer confined to his apartment. She was probably running herself ragged looking at paint colours, furniture or kitchen gadgets! Understandable, because she was not the sort of woman who could sit still.

And yet...

He crooked a finger and the start-up's CEO jumped to attention like a puppet whose strings had been pulled.

He would have to go to Violet. There was no question about it. It took him under a minute to communicate his intentions to his startled sidekick.

'But the signatures still have to hit the paper,' Bob said, frowning. 'Then there's the usual celebrations...'

'Time for you to step up to the plate,' Matt said, looking at his watch and mentally working out how long it would take for him to get to the UK. Private jet or commercial? 'Don't forget the size of the bonus coming your way in a month's time. You can close this deal as efficiently as the next man. Just make sure you keep some of this lot in order and don't let the celebrations run away with you. I expect you back in the UK by the end of the week.'

Commercial, he thought. No time to fuel up and get

things in position. He could be back at his apartment in under ten hours and then he would see for himself just what was going on…

Violet stuffed her mobile under the cushion on the sofa. It had been pinging with messages from Matt. He had tried calling five times. Tough. She wasn't going to answer. She would when her brain stopped whizzing round her head like a helicopter rotor. Just as soon as she started thinking in a straight line. But right now, all she could do was picture an over-the-top bunch of flowers being delivered to some poor, dispatched woman who probably didn't have a clue that her charming billionaire escort was actually sleeping with another woman. Another woman who just happened to be pregnant with his child.

How long had it been going on? Weeks? Months? Had he now decided, since they were getting along very well, that it was time to call off his outside affair? Had his conscience been kick-started because the baby was well on its way, no longer something that was going to happen, but something that was imminent?

She was tortured by questions and in no fit state to talk to him on the telephone.

Typically, he wouldn't give up. Of course, she couldn't bury her head in the sand like an ostrich for ever, but just for the moment, she needed time to think.

She wished she had a mum around. Or at least a good friend, someone she had shared the ups and downs of her life with, who could give her a pep talk, make her a cup of tea and tell her that everything was going to be okay.

No such luck.

A good night's sleep, if she could get it, would have to do the trick. He was due back the following evening, and by then she would have to have found a way through the pain, the whirring head, the clammy hands and the sick feeling in the pit of her stomach.

She hit the sack early and fell into a restless sleep. She couldn't stop thinking. She would have to call quits on whatever relationship they had been trying to cultivate. She'd thought they'd been making progress but she'd obviously been mistaken because behind her back he'd been seeing someone. She reminded herself that she'd originally banked on going it alone. It wouldn't be the end of the world. She would just have to power on—and wasn't it great that at least she wasn't financially dependent on him? Not that he would ever fail to contribute his fair share and beyond.

She thought she'd never fall asleep, but she must have nodded off because she didn't hear the sound of the front door opening. She only realised that Matt had returned when a sliver of light penetrated the darkness, and she groggily surfaced in stages to see his shadowy outline framed by the door.

He was so still that he could have been a statue. Heart thumping, Violet propped herself up on her elbows, then clumsily turned to switch on the light by the bed.

Not for one second did she think that the unexpected appearance was anyone but Matt. Certainly, she could not have mistaken his dauntingly impressive frame for anyone else.

'What's going on?' he demanded without preamble, stepping forward.

'Huh?'

'You haven't been answering my calls.'

'What are you doing here?' Violet's brain finally cranked into gear, but her heart was still beating like a drum and her mouth was dry. 'Shouldn't you be sealing the deal on the opposite side of the world?'

'How could I do that when I was worried sick about you?'

'Oh, please…' She was beginning to think straight and the swirling, muddy waters of all the emotions with which she had gone to bed were right back with her, firing her with fury, disappointment and unhappiness.

'What is that supposed to mean?'

'As if you don't know, Matt,' Violet muttered under her breath.

'I don't know.'

The silence stretched to a breaking point between them. She had planned to handle this situation in a very different way. For a start, she had decided that anything but an adult approach wasn't going to do. She had pretty much determined that she wouldn't mention the good-bye flowers at all. She would simply tell him that they had experimented with the concept of living together and she felt that she would not be able to continue it.

She toyed with the idea of telling him that she had feelings for him. That would certainly do the trick when it came to getting him to catapult himself off the starting block at great speed. But then she realised that she would have to live with him feeling sorry for her for ever, even if she moved on to find someone else.

Poor Violet... I warned her not to get emotionally involved but she just couldn't help herself...

'The flowers,' she said quietly, and he frowned in puzzlement.

'I need something to drink, Violet. Water. Then we can continue this conversation.'

He spun round on his heels and no sooner had he left the bedroom than she awkwardly heaved herself out of the bed, slung on her dressing gown, belting it securely round her tummy, and followed him into the kitchen.

She didn't want a conversation in bed. She didn't want him sitting on the edge looking at her or, worse, climbing into bed with her to continue their talk. She was realistic enough to know that a bed plus Matt Falconer was a lethal combination when it came to her defence system.

She padded out to find him gulping down a glass of water, his back to her.

'The flowers, Matt,' she repeated, and he turned round and looked at her, simultaneously dumping the empty glass on the counter. 'And don't pretend that you don't know what I'm talking about. Glo called.'

'Glo? Glo who?'

Of course he wouldn't recognise the name, Violet thought bitterly. He'd always left the nuts and bolts of saying goodbye to her to sort out, while he merrily galloped towards another empty affair.

'Glo from the flower shop in Knightsbridge. You know the one. She called to say that you'd started an order for your *usual* but had failed to complete it so she didn't know what you wanted to do with the flowers. If you tell me who the poor girl is, then I can call her back and arrange for them to be sent to her.'

Violet barely needed to see the expression on his face because the absolute stillness of his body was enough to give the game away. He knew what she was talking about and he wasn't going to try to pretend otherwise.

'The flowers,' he said. 'It never occurred to me that the woman would call you.'

'Why would that be? I've been dealing with her for… for years. Together, we've been taking care of all those broken hearts you've left behind, sending flowers as though a bunch of blooms can patch them up and make them good.'

'There's no need for drama, Violet.'

'This is not what I signed up for.'

'You don't understand.'

'Matt, that must be the most well-worn statement any man can make when he's made a mistake and been caught red-handed.' She was managing to keep her voice level, but it came at a cost. Her heart was splintering into a thousand pieces. She looked away and shuffled towards the sofa because her legs felt wobbly.

'Violet…'

His voice was soft right behind her but, when he placed his hand on her arm, she angrily shook it off without looking at him.

'I don't want this for myself, Matt. I don't want *you*.' She sank onto the sofa and didn't look at him as he hovered in front of her, the very essence of a guilt-ridden male, she thought, raking his fingers through his hair, his fabulous eyes not quite able to meet hers… All that was missing was the stammer.

Anger, jealousy, searing hurt all fused inside her and she briefly closed her eyes and breathed in deeply. When she opened them, he was still there, towering over her, arms folded.

'I'm telling you that you don't understand.'

'And I'm telling *you* that I do! I understand because I know you, because I've been down this road before, don't forget! I've arranged the flowers and sent them on your behalf, except this time you were going to send the flowers yourself until you got wrapped up with your deal and forgot.'

'I think I need something a little stronger to drink than water,' he ground out, turning round and heading to the kitchen, to reappear within minutes with a glass of whisky that he downed in one ferocious gulp.

'Please don't try to talk your way out of this, Matt,' she said when he pulled a chair towards her and sat down. 'I deserve the truth and then... Well, we can take things from there, but first and foremost we'll have to agree that this experiment has failed.'

'Please, Violet...'

'Please what? Please try to listen to whatever version of the truth you decide to come out with to placate me? Please accept a situation where I share you with other women? Absolutely not!'

'Do you honestly think that I'm that sort of person?' he demanded, and when she would have turned away he leant forward and tilted her face to his so that she couldn't avoid his searching gaze.

'I didn't,' she said truthfully. 'But, then again, as you once pointed out, we're not married, are we? Some people aren't meant to settle down. They're rolling stones. You're one of those people, Matt, and if I was lulled into thinking otherwise then I'm wide awake now.'

'I can explain...'

Violet looked at him stonily. She had always had her pride, and she had a lot of experience when it came to concealing her emotions from him. She had fancied him from a distance, but he would never have guessed in a million years as she made those phone calls to the flower shop and arranged theatre tickets and opera seats for the women who'd flitted in and out of his life.

She wanted to burst into tears, but there was no way

she was going to do that. Every bone in her body hurt from the effort of keeping it together.

'Please don't bother.'

'Okay, I admit that, yes, I ordered the flowers.'

'I told you that I don't want to hear!' The last thing she needed was an agonised confession of infidelity. He would use his words carefully, but the message would remain the same and it was a message she didn't want to hear. There was only so much reality any person could take in one go.

'But then I chickened out from actually having them delivered.'

'Because you couldn't bear to say goodbye to whoever was on the receiving end?' She clenched her hands into tights fists and stared at him with simmering hostility.

How could so much beauty be so lethal? But then, wasn't nature full of poisonous creatures whose physical appearance could seduce and enchant?

'Because I didn't know how to say hello,' Matt muttered under his breath. She had to strain to catch what he was saying. She was grudgingly riveted because, for the very first time, he was shorn of his usual self-assurance. A dark flush highlighted his cheekbones and he had lowered his eyes. Every muscle in his body shrieked tension.

'What are you talking about?'

'I'm no good at this sort of thing.'

'What sort of thing? Behaving like a decent human

being and telling the truth?' An unfair and uncharitable remark. She knew that. He was a decent human being. He'd been decent from the start and it was all her fault if she'd hoped for more.

'Violet…would you listen to me? Please? No interruption?'

Violet shrugged, but the plea in his voice held her still. He was so assertive, so dominant, that that ghost of a plea momentarily derailed her.

'All of this…us…what happened… None of it… I never predicted any of it.'

'That makes the two of us, Matt,' Violet muttered, flicking resentful eyes at him.

'You handed in your notice, Violet, and I didn't think how much I really relied on you until you did that. I read that email and my blood ran cold. Why do you think I raced over to your house? There was no way I could have waited until the following morning.'

'I don't know what that has to do with anything.'

'No interruption. Remember?' He smiled crookedly at her and she felt her treacherous body melt a little. She sternly reminded herself that melting was not an option.

'I've asked myself whether I would have gone to Melbourne if I hadn't had those deals on the go, if I hadn't had an excuse. The more I realised that I would have, the more I realised just how…dependent I had become on you over the years. It wasn't a message I was happy to take on board, so I did the obvious thing and ignored it.'

Violet was listening intently. She didn't know where this was going, but for the moment she had forgotten all about the flowers and was focused instead on whatever road he was leading her down.

He was so intent, his navy eyes so compelling. Part of her wanted to break away but she was held in place against her will. *Dependent how?* she wanted to ask, but that was a dangerous road to follow, so she focused on telling herself that she'd been a brilliant secretary who could handle him and of course he'd unwittingly become dependent on her. There was no point reading beyond that.

'I saw you on that stage, Violet, and something else I never realised hit me like a sledgehammer.'

'What was that?'

'I wanted you. I was attracted to you. Something about you…went beyond physical attraction, and I never registered that because, for me, there had never been anything beyond physical attraction. Physical attraction was something I could understand. Sex was good, but sex was all there was, and as far as I was concerned it was all there ever would be with any woman. A relationship involved feelings I knew I would never have and I was never going to be in the business of pretending otherwise. I grew up in a house where there was never any demonstration of affection between my parents and I guess what you see becomes learned behaviour. I accepted that without really analysing it. But then you left me.'

'Matt, I hardly *left* you.'

'You left me,' he said gruffly. 'That's what it felt like. I should have known that what I felt weren't the usual feelings of a boss who has lost his brilliant PA— and I certainly should have realised that what I felt was something way deeper the very minute we climbed into bed. Nothing had felt so right, Violet. Everything was magnified. Exquisitely intense. I never wanted it to stop. That should have set the alarm bells ringing, but I'd never heard those bells before, and I had no idea what they signified.'

'Please, Matt, don't say things you don't mean.'

'I wouldn't. When I left Melbourne, I thought life would go back to normal, but it didn't. On the surface, everything was as it should be, but below the surface…a crack had opened, and it grew bigger by the day. There was no way I was conditioned to put two and two together but, when you showed up at my office all those weeks later, I was over the moon.'

'You were?'

'You'd come back. And then you told me that you were pregnant and I was shocked at how readily I accepted the situation. I'd never planned on having a family, yet there I was, and I wasn't complaining half as much as I should have been.'

'Matt…' Violet whispered helplessly.

'I wanted to marry you. I couldn't stand the thought of not having you and our baby in my life on a permanent basis. But you weren't having it and, while I understood where you were coming from, I still couldn't stand it.'

'You stopped asking very quickly,' she pointed out, unwillingly drawn into a conversation that was dangerously seductive.

'I didn't want to scare you off, but then you relented, told me that you were willing to meet me halfway.'

'I hated the thought of you finding someone else,' Violet admitted, breaking all her self-imposed rules about revealing as little as possible. 'I hated thinking that I would see you with another woman hanging on your arm whenever you came round to see our child. I hated the thought that you would probably end up marrying one of those women. Like I've said, a single guy pushing a pram is an irresistible temptation. I also knew, whether I wanted to admit it to myself or not, that two parents were always going to be better together than apart when it came to a child's best interests. You were prepared to be unselfish. Why shouldn't I?'

'Violet…' His voice roughened and he looked away, his body language awkward but intensely appealing in its sincerity. 'The flowers…'

'The flowers.'

'For you.'

'I beg your pardon?'

'The flowers were for you. It took me a while, because I was so bloody slow on the uptake, but I finally slotted all the pieces of the jigsaw together and saw what had been staring me in the face from that very first moment we slept together. I love you, Violet. You, your smile, your quick wit, the way you have of standing your ground and not giving an inch. I love the way you stand up to me. I love the way you make me feel.'

'You *love* me?'

'I didn't recognise the symptoms.' He smiled a hesitant smile and reached forward to link her fingers loosely with his. 'Even though I knew I had a virus.'

'Are you really being honest with me?'

'I would never lie about something like this. I always thought that my heart was firmly locked away, but you managed to get hold of the key…and I think it happened long before we slept together. You have the whole package, Violet, and I was an idiot not to see that sooner.'

Violet's heart was soaring and there was a drumbeat in her ears. 'I love you too, Matt.' It felt a dangerous crossing of lines to utter those words, because she'd spent so long making sure they never left her lips. She almost expected him to pull back, despite everything he had just said, but he didn't. He smiled. She tentatively held her hand against his face and he caught it in his and kissed her palm.

'I was so attracted to you before I left for Melbourne, but I knew that it would never come to anything because we were just so different. The last sort of guy I wanted was someone who played the field, and there was no way you could ever be attracted to me, anyway. I'd seen way too much of the women you went for to ever think that you could go for someone like me.

'Then you came to Melbourne and you were there for me when my father was rushed into hospital. Sleeping with you…felt so incredibly good, but I just looked at it as stolen happiness. It wasn't going to last, but I would hold on to it for as long as I could. When I found out that I was pregnant, I was so confused. I knew I had to tell you, but the thought of seeing you again…scared me. I'm not sure when I realised that I loved you. Maybe I always knew, just as I knew that love was the last thing you would ever want from me.'

She paused. 'Why didn't you send the flowers?'

'I chickened out. I suspected you had feelings for me, but I couldn't be sure. I loved you, but what was that about? How had that happened? I placed the order for forty-eight red roses and then I panicked. Had second thoughts. I told myself that I'd get back to it, make my mind up, take the bull by the horns, but I needed a couple of days to think it through. It never occurred to me that the woman at the flower shop would get in touch with you, but she did, and here we are.

'My darling, darling Violet. We love one another and I have never been happier in my entire life. So, please, will you marry me? Not because we're having a baby, but because we want to share the rest of our lives together.'

'How could I possibly say no to that?'

She smiled at him, then leant forward and pulled him towards her, and the feel of his mouth on hers sent her heart into a crazy tailspin. Oh, how used to that feeling she was—but, oh, how wonderful that this time the feeling was mutual.

They were married less than a month later, plenty of time to have got her father over. Every single employee attended, along with friends from every walk of life, including many of her father's friends, most of whom she remembered well. It was a rowdy and memorable affair. Her father was in his element and, at the end of a brilliant evening, he and some of his former band members formed an impromptu group to play for the newlyweds.

Matt's parents, as stiff-lipped as she had expected, unbent a little by the end of the evening. This time, when his mother politely repeated her invitation to lunch, Violet nodded and conceded that it might not be quite as bad as she had reckoned the first time the invitation had been extended.

Who knew? Maybe a baby would change the dynamics.

They should have had a honeymoon of her choosing, Matt had said, but with his usual overprotective gene in full flow, he had put his foot down at any destination that involved a plane. She was far too pregnant to travel, he had determined, even if the duration of the flight was ten seconds.

So they had a romantic week in deepest Cornwall, where the weather pretty much did what they wanted it to. They had lovely walks and a roaring fire in the evening.

And then, in the blink of an eye, Matilda was there. Eight pounds six ounces of curly black hair, navy-blue eyes, a rosebud mouth and little chubby hands punching the air.

Now, six months later, Violet could smile at the memory of just how panicked Matt had been when she had gone into labour.

Her cool, collected and self-assured husband had been at his most flustered.

'Just remember to breathe,' she had told him, amused and indulgent in between contractions, 'and you'll be okay.'

She heard the sound of the front door opening, but this time it wasn't the door to his apartment, but the door to the house on Richmond Hill where they now lived. They had finally opted for somewhere close enough for Matt to return home in the evenings in time to see Matilda before she went to bed. Original plans to move farther out had been put on the back burner.

He strode in and was as mesmerising as he always was, walking towards her with that slow smile that still made her toes curl and her skin prickle with love and desire.

'An early Friday,' he drawled, kissing her on the mouth and then kissing her again before pulling back. 'As instructed by my darling wife.' He glanced past her from hallway to open-plan kitchen. 'And I see the table is set for…' He frowned. 'For five people?'

'I thought I'd surprise you,' Violet said, pulling him

towards the kitchen. Matilda was sound asleep in her cot and she could sense that he was itching to go in and have a look at his sleeping daughter. 'My dad's coming over for dinner...and your parents.'

'My *parents*?'

'Why not?'

'Why not, indeed?' he murmured. 'What time are they over?'

'We have a couple of hours. They won't be here until seven forty-five.'

'In that case...' He leant down to brush his mouth against her neck and, at the same time, he curved a possessive hand underneath the short-sleeved jumper to find the swell of her naked breasts, because she was braless. On cue, he hardened, and even more so when he pushed up the jumper to tease her nipple between his fingers. 'We have plenty of time for me to look in on Matilda and then have ourselves a little bit of fun... wouldn't you agree?'

Violet smiled. Yes, she would agree. She tiptoed to curl her hands around his neck and pulled him to her so that she could kiss him, a long, lingering kiss, full of love, desire and adoration.

She most certainly would agree.

* * * * *

If you fell in love with
His Secretary's Nine-Month Notice,
Cathy Williams's 100th book
for Harlequin Presents,
you're sure to adore these
other stories by the author!

Contracted for the Spaniard's Heir
Marriage Bargain with His Innocent
Shock Marriage for the Powerful Spaniard
The Italian's Christmas Proposition

Available now!

WE HOPE YOU ENJOYED
THIS BOOK FROM
 HARLEQUIN
PRESENTS

Escape to exotic locations where passion knows no bounds.

Welcome to the glamorous lives of royals and billionaires, where passion knows no bounds. Be swept into a world of luxury, wealth and exotic locations.

8 NEW BOOKS AVAILABLE EVERY MONTH!

HPHALO2020

COMING NEXT MONTH FROM

HARLEQUIN
PRESENTS

Available May 19, 2020

#3817 CINDERELLA'S ROYAL SECRET
Once Upon a Temptation
by Lynne Graham
For innocent cleaner Izzy, accidentally interrupting her most exclusive client, Sheikh Rafiq, coming out of the shower is mortifying...yet their instantaneous attraction leads to the most amazing night of her life! But then she does a pregnancy test...

#3818 BEAUTY AND HER ONE-NIGHT BABY
Once Upon a Temptation
by Dani Collins
The first time Scarlett sees Javiero after their impassioned night together, she's in labor with his baby! She won't accept empty vows, even if she can't forget the pleasure they shared...and could share again!

#3819 SHY QUEEN IN THE ROYAL SPOTLIGHT
Once Upon a Temptation
by Natalie Anderson
To retain the throne he's sacrificed everything for, Alek *must* choose a bride. Hester's inner fire catches his attention. Alek sees the queen that she could truly become—but the real question is, can *she*?

#3820 CLAIMED IN THE ITALIAN'S CASTLE
Once Upon a Temptation
by Caitlin Crews
When innocent piano-playing Angelina must marry enigmatic Benedetto Franceschi, she *should* be terrified—his reputation precedes him. But their electrifying chemistry forges an unspoken connection. Dare she hope he could become the husband she deserves?

HPCNMRA0520

#3821 EXPECTING HIS BILLION-DOLLAR SCANDAL
Once Upon a Temptation
by Cathy Williams
Luca relished the fact his fling with Cordelia was driven by desire,
not his wealth. Now their baby compels him to bring her into his
sumptuous world. But to give Cordelia his heart? It's a price he
can't pay...

#3822 TAMING THE BIG BAD BILLIONAIRE
Once Upon a Temptation
by Pippa Roscoe
Ella may be naive, but she's no pushover. Discovering Roman's
lies, she can't pretend their passion-filled marriage never
happened. He might see himself as a big bad wolf, but she knows
he could be so much more...

#3823 THE FLAW IN HIS MARRIAGE PLAN
Once Upon a Temptation
by Tara Pammi
Family is *everything* to tycoon Vincenzo. The man who ruined
his mother's life will pay. Vincenzo will wed his enemy's adopted
daughter: Alessandra. The flaw in his plan? Their fiery attraction...
and his need to protect her.

#3824 HIS INNOCENT'S PASSIONATE AWAKENING
Once Upon a Temptation
by Melanie Milburne
If there's a chance that marrying Artie will give his grandfather
the will to live, Luca *must* do it. But he's determined to resist
temptation. Until their scorching wedding kiss stirs the beauty to
sensual new life! _____

**YOU CAN FIND MORE INFORMATION ON UPCOMING HARLEQUIN TITLES,
FREE EXCERPTS AND MORE AT HARLEQUIN.COM.**

HPCNMRB0520

SPECIAL EXCERPT FROM

HHARLEQUIN
PRESENTS

*The first time Scarlett sees Javiero after their
impassioned night together she's in labour with his
baby! But she won't accept empty vows—even if she
can't forget the pleasure they shared...and could
share again!*

*Read on for a sneak preview of Dani Collins's
next story for Harlequin Presents,*
Beauty and Her One-Night Baby.

Scarlett dropped her phone with a clatter.

She had been trying to call Kiara. Now she was taking in the
livid claw marks across Javiero's face, each pocked on either side
with the pinpricks of recently removed stitches. His dark brown
hair was longer than she'd ever seen it, perhaps gelled back from
the widow's peak at some point this morning, but it was mussed
and held a jagged part. He wore a black eye patch like a pirate, its
narrow band cutting a thin stripe across his temple and into his hair.

Maybe that's why his features looked as though they had been
set askew? His mouth was...not right. His upper lip was uneven
and the claw marks drew lines through his unkempt stubble all the
way down into his neck.

That was dangerously close to his jugular! Dear God, he had
nearly been killed.

She grasped at the edge of the sink, trying to stay on her feet
while she grew so light-headed at the thought of him dying that she
feared she would faint.

The ravages of his attack weren't what made him look so
forbidding and grim, though, she computed through her haze of

panic and anguish. No. The contemptuous glare in his one eye was for her. For this.

He flicked another outraged glance at her middle.

"I thought we were meeting in the boardroom." His voice sounded gravelly. Damaged as well? Or was that simply his true feelings toward her now? Deadly and completely devoid of any of the sensual admiration she'd sometimes heard in his tone.

Not that he'd ever been particularly warm toward her. He'd been aloof, indifferent, irritated, impatient, explosively passionate. Generous in the giving of pleasure. Of compliments. Then cold as she left. Disapproving. Malevolent.

Damningly silent.

And now he was…what? Ignoring that she was as big as a barn?

Her arteries were on fire with straight adrenaline, her heart pounding and her brain spinning with the way she was having to switch gears so fast. Her eyes were hot and her throat tight. Everything in her wanted to scream *help me*, but she'd been in enough tight spots to know this was all on her. Everything was always on her. She fought to keep her head and get through the next few minutes before she moved on to the next challenge.

Which was just a tiny trial called childbirth, but she would worry about that when she got to the hospital.

As the tingle of a fresh contraction began to pang in her lower back, she tightened her grip on the edge of the sink and gritted her teeth, trying to ignore the coming pain and hang on to what dregs of dignity she had left.

"I'm in labor," she said tightly. "It's yours."

Don't miss
Beauty and Her One-Night Baby.

Available June 2020 wherever
Harlequin Presents books and ebooks are sold.

Harlequin.com

Copyright © 2020 by Dani Collins

HPEXP0520

Get 4 FREE REWARDS!

We'll send you 2 FREE Books plus 2 FREE Mystery Gifts.

HARLEQUIN PRESENTS

Indian Prince's Hidden Son
USA TODAY BESTSELLING AUTHOR
LYNNE GRAHAM

HARLEQUIN PRESENTS

The Greek's One-Night Heir
USA TODAY BESTSELLING AUTHOR
NATALIE ANDERSON

Harlequin Presents books feature the glamorous lives of royals and billionaires in a world of exotic locations, where passion knows no bounds.

FREE Value Over **$20**

YES! Please send me 2 FREE Harlequin Presents novels and my 2 FREE gifts (gifts are worth about $10 retail). After receiving them, if I don't wish to receive any more books, I can return the shipping statement marked "cancel." If I don't cancel, I will receive 6 brand-new novels every month and be billed just $4.55 each for the regular-print edition or $5.80 each for the larger-print edition in the U.S., or $5.49 each for the regular-print edition or $5.99 each for the larger-print edition in Canada. That's a savings of at least 11% off the cover price! It's quite a bargain! Shipping and handling is just 50¢ per book in the U.S. and $1.25 per book in Canada.* I understand that accepting the 2 free books and gifts places me under no obligation to buy anything. I can always return a shipment and cancel at any time. The free books and gifts are mine to keep no matter what I decide.

Choose one: ☐ **Harlequin Presents Regular-Print** (106/306 HDN GNWY) ☐ **Harlequin Presents Larger-Print** (176/376 HDN GNWY)

Name (please print)

Address   Apt. #

City   State/Province   Zip/Postal Code

Mail to the Reader Service:
IN U.S.A.: P.O. Box 1341, Buffalo, NY 14240-8531
IN CANADA: P.O. Box 603, Fort Erie, Ontario L2A 5X3

Want to try 2 free books from another series? Call 1-800-873-8635 or visit www.ReaderService.com.

*Terms and prices subject to change without notice. Prices do not include sales taxes, which will be charged (if applicable) based on your state or country of residence. Canadian residents will be charged applicable taxes. Offer not valid in Quebec. This offer is limited to one order per household. Books received may not be as shown. Not valid for current subscribers to Harlequin Presents books. All orders subject to approval. Credit or debit balances in a customer's account(s) may be offset by any other outstanding balance owed by or to the customer. Please allow 4 to 6 weeks for delivery. Offer available while quantities last.

Your Privacy—The Reader Service is committed to protecting your privacy. Our Privacy Policy is available online at www.ReaderService.com or upon request from the Reader Service. We make a portion of our mailing list available to reputable third parties that offer products we believe may interest you. If you prefer that we not exchange your name with third parties, or if you wish to clarify or modify your communication preferences, please visit us at www.ReaderService.com/consumerschoice or write to us at Reader Service Preference Service, P.O. Box 9062, Buffalo, NY 14240-9062. Include your complete name and address.

HP20R

**IF YOU ENJOYED THIS BOOK
WE THINK YOU WILL ALSO LOVE**

HARLEQUIN
DESIRE

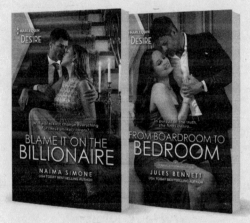

*Luxury, scandal, desire—welcome to
the lives of the American elite.*

Be transported to the worlds of oil barons, family dynasties,
moguls and celebrities. Get ready for juicy plot twists,
delicious sensuality and intriguing scandal.

6 NEW BOOKS AVAILABLE EVERY MONTH!

HDXSERIES2020

Love Harlequin romance?

DISCOVER.
Be the first to find out about promotions, news and exclusive content!

Facebook.com/HarlequinBooks

Twitter.com/HarlequinBooks

Instagram.com/HarlequinBooks

Pinterest.com/HarlequinBooks

ReaderService.com

EXPLORE.
Sign up for the Harlequin e-newsletter and download a free book from any series at **TryHarlequin.com**

CONNECT.
Join our Harlequin community to share your thoughts and connect with other romance readers!
Facebook.com/groups/HarlequinConnection

HSOCIAL2020